## ALSO BY THOMAS FASANO

*The Dead (editor)*
*Great Short Stories by Great American Writers (editor)*
*Common Core Grammar: High School Edition*
*The Arean Wall*
*Luminance*
*Receipt of Days*
*Snowline and Other Distances*
*Landfill*
*Forsaken Hymns*
*Harold Redux*
*Colossians: Verse-By-Verse Graphic Novel (illustrator)*

**Thomas Fasano**

# Venice Beach Psalms

COYOTE CANYON PRESS  CLAREMONT, CALIFORNIA www.coyotecanyonpress.com

ISBN: 979-8-9877655-7-9

# Venice Beach Psalms

# Chapter 1: The Client

**Three days sober.**

Not much of a streak, I know. But it's what I had. Three days of coffee instead of whiskey, shaking hands instead of steady lies, AA meetings instead of bar stools. Three days of being Peter Blair, private investigator, instead of Peter Blair, professional fuck-up.

The distinction gets blurry.

My office smelled like old coffee and new regret. Second floor walkup in Echo Park, the kind of place where the rent's cheap because hope died here decades ago. Through my window I could see the taco stand across the street doing decent business, and the check-cashing place doing better. The city had its priorities straight.

I was nursing my fourth cup of the morning when Declan Fury walked through my door.

Recognized him immediately. Hard not to. We'd shared some AA meetings over the years, him and me. Never talked much—you don't, not really, just nod and acknowledge the mutual damage. But I knew him. Declan Fury. Lead singer of The Fury back when punk rock meant something and Reagan was president. One gold album, a thousand bad decisions, eight years sober.

He looked like death's demo tape.

Tall, gaunt, gray mohawk that might've been ironic in 1983 but just looked desperate now. Leather jacket worn through at the elbows. The kind of face that's earned every line. Missing two fingers on his left hand—stage accident, someone told me once. The price of authenticity.

"Blair," he said.

"Fury."

He stood there, hesitating. People always hesitate before they hire a PI. Like admitting they need help is the final surrender. I waited. Waiting's free.

"You know who I am," he said.

"Saw you at the Tuesday night meeting. Koreatown."

"Yeah." He moved further into the room, looking at the filing cabinet I never use, the client chair that wobbles, the water stain on the ceiling that resembles California if you're drunk enough. "You probably heard about The Fury. The band."

"Before my time. But yeah."

A ghost of a smile. "Everyone says that now."

I gestured to the unstable chair. He sat. I stayed behind my desk because furniture's the only authority I've got left.

"What can I do for you?"

He pulled out a photo. Handed it across the desk. Young woman, early twenties, dark hair, sharp features. Pretty in that way that makes the world dangerous. She had his eyes.

"My daughter. Siobhan."

Irish name. Pronounced Shiv-awn. His accent made it sound like music.

"She's missing," he continued. "Three weeks now."

I studied the photo. Girl looked alive in it. Smiling at whoever took the picture. Vintage band t-shirt, multiple piercings, the uniform of searching for yourself in other people's styles.

"You go to the police?"

"Yeah. They took a report. Said she's an adult, has a right to disappear." He leaned forward, and I saw the tremor in his hands. Not booze. Fear. "But she wouldn't. Not like this."

They all say that. Sometimes they're right.

"Tell me about her."

He took a breath. Gathered his words like picking up pieces of broken glass.

"Twenty-three. Smart. Troubled. Her mother died two years ago. Cancer. Siobhan took it hard. We weren't close before that—my fault, a thousand reasons I won't bore you with—but after, we tried. Started talking. She moved out here from Sacramento. Got a place in Mar Vista, worked at some coffee shop in Venice."

"What changed?"

"About a month ago, she got weird. Distant. Stopped answering calls. Her roommate said she was obsessed with some street preacher. Started spending all her time at the beach with this guy's... I don't know what to call it. Ministry? Cult? She stopped going to work, stopped paying rent." He pulled out his phone, showed me a text message. "This is the last thing she sent me."

*Found something real. Don't worry.*

Famous last words of the lost.

"You know this preacher's name?"

"Emmett something. Cain, I think. Calls himself Prophet Emmett."

Of course he does.

I sat back in my chair. It squeaked. Everything in my office announces failure.

"Mr. Fury—"

"Declan."

"Declan. Missing persons, especially adults... it's messy. Most of the time they don't want to be found. And if she's involved with some religious group, she might be there voluntarily."

"I know that." His voice tight. "I know what voluntary looks like. I spent twenty years volunteering for my own destruction. This is different. She's in trouble. I can feel it."

Father's intuition. Sometimes it's bullshit. Sometimes it's the only truth available.

"Venice Beach is complicated territory," I said. "Homeless crisis, drugs, exploitation. If this Cain character is running something down there, it could be dangerous."

"That's why I need you."

"I'm expensive." Lie. I'm cheap. But rent's due and my Honda needs new brake pads.

He pulled out an envelope. Put it on my desk. I didn't touch it yet.

"Five hundred," he said. "Cash. It's what I have. I can get more. Somehow."

I looked at him. Recovering addict, aging punk rocker, working some shit job at a record store probably, trying to save a daughter he barely knew. Five hundred was everything.

"Keep the extra," I said. "Five hundred covers a week."

Relief washed over his face like absolution.

"You'll find her?"

I never promise that. Promises are for people who don't know better.

"I'll look. If she's in Venice, I'll find her. What happens after that…" I shrugged. "Depends on what I find."

He nodded. Understood the limitations. In recovery, you learn not to control outcomes.

"There's something else," he said, and his voice dropped. "The last time I saw her, she said something. About her mom. About how she'd found the family her mom wanted her to have. Like this Cain guy was giving her something I couldn't."

Purpose. Belonging. The things we sell ourselves for.

"I'll start today," I told him. "I'll need her address, her room-mate's name, the coffee shop where she worked. Anywhere else she spent time."

He gave me everything. Wrote it down on the back of a flyer for some concert that happened in 1986. His handwriting was terrible, musician's scrawl, but I could read it. Barely.

We stood. Shook hands. His grip was firm despite the trem-or.

"Thank you," he said.

"Don't thank me yet."

He left. The door closed. I sat back down and looked at the envelope. Five hundred dollars. Siobhan Fury's photo. A street preacher named Prophet Emmett Cain.

I opened my bottom desk drawer. Looked at the bottle of Jameson I kept there. For clients, I told myself. Always for clients.

Closed the drawer.

Opened the envelope instead.
I took his money. I took his hope.
Same thing, really.

# Chapter 2: The Regular Routes

**The 10 Freeway west was a parking lot at eleven a.m.**

Typical LA. Traffic like a blood clot, everyone going nowhere fast. I had the Honda's windows down because the AC died last summer and I couldn't afford to fix it. Hot air and exhaust fumes. The smell of ambition stuck in neutral.

Joan Didion wrote about freeway music. The rhythm of movement and stasis. She understood this city better than anyone. Knew that LA was all about the going, not the arriving. I was going to Mar Vista to talk to Siobhan Fury's roommate. Whether I'd arrive at anything useful remained to be seen.

The address Declan gave me was a small apartment complex off Centinela. Two stories, stucco the color of old teeth, palm trees that had seen better decades. Rent here probably ran two grand a month for a one-bedroom. The new LA math: work three jobs, live with strangers, call it freedom.

I parked in a spot marked VISITOR. Climbed exterior stairs that smelled like someone's morning weed. Apartment 2C.

Knocked.

The door opened on a chain. Young woman, mid-twenties, blonde hair in a messy bun, suspicious eyes.

"Yeah?"

"Jessica? I'm Peter Blair. I called earlier about Siobhan."

"You're the private detective."

"Private investigator. Detectives get pensions."

She didn't smile. Closed the door, unlatched the chain, opened it again. Stepped back to let me in.

The apartment was small and clean. Ikea furniture, posters for bands I'd never heard of, plants struggling in inadequate light. Two bedrooms off the main room. One door open, one closed.

"That was hers," Jessica said, pointing to the closed door. "I haven't touched anything. Feels weird, you know? Like she's dead or something."

"She's not dead."

"You know that for sure?"

"No."

She sat on the couch. I took the chair across from her. Between us, a coffee table with fashion magazines and empty coffee cups. The archaeology of young lives.

"How long did you live together?" I asked.

"About a year. Found each other on Craigslist. She seemed cool. Was cool, actually. We got along."

"Until?"

"Until about a month ago. She got weird."

"Weird how?"

Jessica pulled her knees up, wrapped her arms around them. Defensive posture. Whatever happened, she felt guilty about it.

"She met this guy. Street preacher down in Venice. Started going to his... I don't know what to call it. Services? Gatherings? She'd come home all hyped up, talking about community and purpose and finding her real family."

"What did you think?"

"I thought it was bullshit. Told her so. We fought about it." She looked away. "I should've been nicer. She'd lost her mom. She was hurting. But it felt so obviously like a con, you know?"

"Did you meet this preacher? Emmett Cain?"

"Once. He came here to pick her up. Gave me the creeps. Too friendly. Too interested. The kind of guy who makes eye contact like he's trying to read your soul."

I knew the type. Charisma as camouflage.

"What happened after the fight?"

"She moved out. Not officially. Just stopped coming home. I'd text her, she'd say she was staying with friends, with the 'family.' Stopped paying her share of rent. Stopped showing up for her shifts at the coffee shop. Three weeks ago, I went to Venice to find her. Saw her at one of Cain's gatherings. She looked right through me. Like I was nobody."

Her voice cracked. She cleared her throat, tried to hold it together.

"That's when I knew she was gone."

"Gone how?"

"Brainwashed. Programmed. Whatever you call it when someone stops being themselves." She looked at me directly. "Her dad hired you?"

"Yeah."

"Good. He actually gives a shit, at least."

"You don't think so?"

"I don't know. She never talked about him much. Said he was absent when she was growing up. Too busy being a rock star and a drunk. But after her mom died, they started talking. She wanted to believe in him." Jessica stood, paced to the window. "I wanted to believe in her. Thought she'd snap out of it. Thought she'd come home."

"Can I see her room?"

She nodded. Led me to the closed door. Opened it.

The room was small. Single bed, desk, closet. Clothes still hanging. Books stacked on the desk and floor. I scanned the titles: Sylvia Plath, Joan Didion, some self-help books about grief and healing. A journal, closed, next to the bed.

"Can I look through this?"

"I guess. I mean, she's missing. Privacy doesn't seem like the priority."

I picked up the journal. Flipped through pages. Her handwriting was small, precise. Entries dated back six months. I skimmed, looking for patterns.

Early entries: grief, confusion, anger at her mother's death. Missing her. Feeling lost in LA.

Then, about six weeks ago, the tone shifted.

*Met someone today who actually listens. Prophet Emmett. He sees people. Really sees them. Talked for hours about purpose and belonging.*

A week later:

*Went to the gathering. It's not like church. It's real. People caring for each other. No judgment. No bullshit. Jessica doesn't understand. She's trapped in the old way of thinking.*

Two weeks after that:

*Moving in with the family soon. Emmett says I'm ready. Says I've been chosen. Finally feel like I belong somewhere.*

The last entry, three weeks ago:

*This is it. This is what Mom wanted for me. Real community. Real love. Surrender feels like freedom.*

I closed the journal. Looked around the room. Saw a young woman searching for meaning in a city that specializes in selling it. Found a man who promised everything and probably delivered nothing.

"She was vulnerable," I said.

"We're all vulnerable. Not all of us join cults."

Fair point.

"Did she have other friends? People she was close to?"

"Not really. She was kind of a loner. Worked, came home, read. We'd get drinks sometimes, but she wasn't much of a drinker." Jessica paused. "Not like me. I can put them away."

Kindred spirit.

"The coffee shop where she worked. You know the name?"

"Venice Grind. On Abbot Kinney. Hipster place. Seven-dollar lattes, you know the type."

I knew the type.

"One more thing," I said. "Did Siobhan ever mention Cain asking for money? Or wanting her to work for the ministry?"

Jessica thought about it. "Not directly. But she talked about 'contributing to the family.' Said everyone had to do their part. I got the feeling it was more than just showing up."

It always was.

I gave Jessica my card. Told her to call if Siobhan reached out. She said she would, but we both knew it was unlikely. When people get swallowed by something bigger, they don't call back to their old lives.

Walking back to my car, I thought about the journal entries. The progression. The seduction. Emmett Cain knew what he was doing. Find the wounded. Offer belonging. Extract everything.

I'd seen it before. In AA meetings, in churches, in relationships. The pattern was always the same.

The difference was what they wanted in return.

I needed to find out what Prophet Emmett Cain was really selling.

And what it cost.

# Chapter 3: Coffee and Questions

**Abbot Kinney Boulevard used to be a place where artists went broke.**

Now it's where tech money goes to feel authentic.

I parked three blocks away because street parking in Venice is a blood sport. Walked past boutiques selling two-hundred-dollar t-shirts and galleries showcasing installations I didn't understand. The old Venice—the Beats and the bikers and the broken—was still there if you knew where to look. But it was buried under artisanal everything and venture capital.

Venice Grind sat between a vintage furniture store and a place that sold crystals. Big windows, reclaimed wood, Edison bulbs. The aesthetic of poverty repurposed for people who'd never experienced it.

I walked in. The smell hit first. Fresh coffee, baking bread, expensive lives. The place was half-full. Laptops open, screenwriters writing screenplays that would never get made, tech bros taking meetings, beautiful people being beautiful.

The counter was marble. The menu was written in chalk. The prices made my wallet hurt.

A kid behind the register—early twenties, man bun, carefully groomed stubble—gave me the customer service smile that meant nothing.

"What can I get you?"

"Coffee. Black. And a minute with the manager."

The smile faltered. "Is there a problem?"

"Just need to ask some questions. You the manager?"

"Assistant manager. Kyle's in the back. Let me grab him."

He disappeared through a door marked EMPLOYEES ONLY. I looked around while I waited. Exposed brick. Succulents in geometric planters. A chalkboard announcing single-origin beans from Guatemala. The kind of place that made coffee a lifestyle choice instead of a survival tool.

Kyle emerged. Thirty-something, same aesthetic as the kid but with more authority. Beard fuller, eyes more tired. He'd been doing this longer and it showed.

"Help you?"

I showed him my investigator's license. "Peter Blair. I'm looking into the disappearance of Siobhan Fury. Heard she worked here."

His expression shifted. Guarded now. "You a cop?"

"Private investigator. Ex-LAPD."

"Helluva beard for an ex-cop."

"I stopped shaving years ago."

"Who hired you?"

"Her father."

He considered this. Nodded.

"Yeah, she worked here. Good employee. Until she wasn't."

"Can we talk?"

He glanced around the café.

"Give me five minutes. Order something and wait."

He disappeared again. I ordered the cheapest thing on the menu—a drip coffee that cost five dollars. The kid made it like he was performing surgery. Handed it to me in a ceramic cup with a perfect foam leaf on top.

"Six-fifty," he said.

"The menu said five."

"Plus tax."

Of course.

I paid. Found a table in the corner. Sipped the coffee. It was good. Probably not six-fifty good, but what did I know. I was used to coffee that came from diners and gas stations and thermoses in my office that hadn't been cleaned since the Clinton administration.

Kyle came out ten minutes later. Sat across from me.

"So Siobhan," he said.

"Tell me about her."

"Hired her about eight months ago. She was reliable. Quiet. Good with customers. Showed up on time, did her work, didn't complain about the usual bullshit."

"What changed?"

"About six weeks ago, she started coming in late. Looking spacey. Tired. I asked if everything was okay. She said she'd found something important. Something real. The way she said it..." He shook his head. "Like she'd joined a pyramid scheme or found Jesus or both."

"Did she mention a name? Emmett Cain?"

"Not at first. But yeah, eventually. Prophet Emmett. She talked about him like he was Gandhi and Tony Robbins combined. Said he was helping people. Building community. All that guru shit."

"You meet him?"

"Once. He came in here. Ordered water—didn't pay for anything—and waited for Siobhan's shift to end. I watched them through the window. The way he looked at her..." Kyle's jaw tightened. "Predatory. That's the word. But she was eating it up."

"Describe him."

"Forties, maybe. Long hair, beard. Dressed like he shopped at thrift stores, but it looked intentional, you know? Like poverty as performance. Handsome in that weathered way. Good posture. Great eye contact. The kind of guy who makes you feel like you're the only person in the room."

Textbook charisma. The most dangerous kind.

"What happened after that?"

"She started missing shifts. Called in sick, except I knew she wasn't sick. She was with him. With his people. I gave her warnings. She apologized, promised to do better, then didn't. Eventually stopped showing up altogether. Stopped answering her phone. I had to let her go. Well, technically she quit by disappearing."

"When was the last time you saw her?"

Kyle thought about it. "Three weeks, maybe? She came in during someone else's shift. Looked different. Thinner. Wearing clothes that weren't hers. Still had that spacey look. Like she was happy but somewhere else."

"Did you talk to her?"

"Tried. She was polite but distant. Said she was doing great. Found her real family. Didn't need the job anymore. The family would take care of her." He leaned back, crossed his arms. "I've seen a lot of people come through Venice. Trust-fund kids playing poor. Addicts playing sober. Everyone playing something. But this felt different. This felt like she'd been re-programmed."

Reprogrammed. Same word Jessica used.

"You know where Cain operates? Where he preaches?"

"Down by the canals, I think. And definitely on the beach. Near the encampments off Rose Avenue. He's always around the homeless population. Claims he's helping them."

"You don't think he is?"

Kyle gave me a look. "This is Venice. Nobody helps any-body without wanting something back. Especially guys who call themselves prophets."

Hard to argue with that.

"Did Siobhan ever mention giving him money? Or work-ing for the ministry in any way?"

"Not directly. But she talked about 'contributing.' Doing her part for the family. I got the impression it wasn't optional."

There it was again. Contribution. The gentle language of exploitation.

I finished my overpriced coffee. Stood to leave. Kyle stood too.

"You think you can find her?" he asked.

"I'm going to try."

"If you do... tell her we'd take her back. If she wanted. The job, I mean. She was good at it."

Small kindness in a hard city. I told him I would.

Walking back to my car, I thought about Emmett Cain. The pieces were assembling. Charismatic leader. Vulnerable follow-ers. Vague talk of contribution and family. Operating in the gray spaces between legitimate ministry and something darker.

I'd been a cop long enough to recognize a con.
The question was what kind of con.
And how deep Siobhan Fury had gone into it.
Time to meet the Prophet.

# Chapter 4: The Boardwalk

**Venice Beach was selling itself like it always did.**

Muscle Beach with bodybuilders pumping iron for tourists. Street performers juggling fire and chainsaws and low expectations. Vendors hawking t-shirts that said things like VENICE BEACH and I SURVIVED VENICE BEACH and other variations on the same lie. Nobody survived Venice. You just passed through or got stuck.

The boardwalk was packed. Midday sun burning everything white and bright. Skateboarders weaving through crowds. Homeless people camped against walls with cardboard signs and empty cups. Tourists from everywhere taking photos of everything.

Two cities occupying the same space. One here for vacation. One with nowhere else to go.

I walked south, toward the Rose Avenue encampments Kyle mentioned. The energy shifted the further I got from the tourist center. Fewer performers. More tents. The smell changed— salt air mixed with unwashed bodies and desperation.

Behind a chain-link fence, someone had set up a village. Maybe forty tents, tarps, shopping carts, the architecture of displacement. People moving between shelters. Some looking destroyed. Some looking surprisingly normal. All looking invisible to everyone walking past.

I stood there, trying to figure my approach. Couldn't just walk into an encampment asking questions. That's how you got nowhere fast. Needed a connection. Someone who worked the area. Someone the residents trusted.

Found them twenty yards away.

A van parked on the street. White, unmarked except for a hand-painted sign: VENICE OUTREACH. Tables set up beside it with sandwiches, bottles of water, basic supplies. A woman in her forties handing out food and talking to a man who looked like sixty years of hard miles.

I waited until she finished her conversation. Approached carefully.

"Excuse me."

She turned. Latina, tired eyes, capable hands. The kind of person who'd heard every story and stopped being surprised.

"If you're hungry, help yourself," she said, gesturing to the table.

"I'm looking for someone."

Her expression hardened. "Cop?"

"Private investigator."

"Same thing."

"Not really. Cops get pensions."

She didn't smile. I wasn't charming her.

"Who are you looking for?"

"Missing woman. Twenty-three. Her name's Siobhan Fury."

I showed her the photo on my phone.

She glanced at it. "Don't know her."

"She was hanging around with a street preacher. Emmett Cain. You know him?"

Her whole body language shifted. Protective. Defensive.

"I know Emmett."

"What do you think of him?"

"I think you should talk to him yourself if you have questions."

"That's the plan. Just trying to get a sense of things first."

She looked at me hard. Weighing whether I was worth the effort. Finally: "What's your name?"

"Peter Blair."

"I'm Ramirez. I do outreach here three days a week. Food, supplies, referrals to services. Been doing it five years."

"Long time."

"Not long enough. This crisis didn't start yesterday."

I nodded. Didn't argue. Wasn't here for politics.

"The missing woman," I said. "Her father hired me. She got involved with Cain's group about a month ago. Stopped contact with everyone. I'm trying to find her."

"Maybe she doesn't want to be found."

"Maybe. But her father deserves to know she's okay."

Ramirez crossed her arms. "Emmett runs a ministry for people who've got nothing. Gives them community. Purpose. A place to belong. The city won't help them. The police won't help them. But Emmett does."

"You trust him?"

She hesitated. That hesitation told me more than her words.

"He helps people," she said finally. "I've seen it. People off the street. Clean. Hopeful. He does good work."

"But?"

"But nothing. You want to know about him, ask him yourself."

"Where can I find him?"

"He holds gatherings at dusk. Down by the canals. Dell Avenue, near the bridge. You'll see the crowd."

"Thanks."

I turned to leave. She stopped me.

"Blair."

I looked back.

"Your missing woman. If she's with Emmett, and she's there voluntarily, you won't be able to just take her. He's got people. They're loyal. And they don't like outsiders."

"Noted."

"I mean it. Tread careful."

I told her I would.

Walked back toward the boardwalk, thinking about Ramirez. Social worker type. Genuine care for the homeless population. But that hesitation when I asked if she trusted Cain. Like she wanted to believe in him but couldn't quite get there.

I had a few hours before dusk. Spent them walking Venice. Getting the lay of the land. The canals were beautiful in that manufactured way—narrow waterways lined with expensive houses, ducks floating past million-dollar real estate. The kind of beauty that cost more than most people made in a year.

Found Dell Avenue. Found the bridge. Saw the spot where a crowd might gather. Quiet now. Just water and architecture and the ghosts of what Venice used to be.

Raymond Chandler wrote about Bay City in his novels. Based it on Venice. Called it a place where "the ocean made no sound at all" and "the whole damned patrol force" was dirty. He understood: scratch the surface of paradise, find the rot underneath.

I bought a cup of coffee from a food truck. Sat on a bench. Waited.

The sun started dropping. The light went golden, then orange, then that particular LA purple that makes everything look significant.

They came in ones and twos. Young people mostly. Some older. All with that searching look. The look of people who'd lost something and hoped to find it here. They gathered near the bridge. Thirty people. Forty. Sitting on the grass, on the concrete, standing in loose clusters.

And then he arrived.

Emmett Cain.

Even from a distance, I could feel it. The presence. The magnetism. He moved through the crowd and they parted for him. Touched shoulders, made eye contact, spoke quiet words that made people light up.

Tall. Lean. Long hair and beard like a Renaissance painting. Simple clothes—jeans, white t-shirt, work boots. Nothing special. Everything calculated.

He stood at the center of the gathering. People sat down. Got quiet. Waited.

I stayed on my bench. Far enough to observe. Close enough to hear.

"Family," he began. His voice was warm. Gentle. The kind of voice that made you want to trust it. "Thank you for being here. Thank you for choosing this. Choosing us. Choosing love over fear."

People nodded. Murmured agreement.

"The world out there wants you small," Cain continued. "Wants you afraid. Wants you alone. They build systems to keep you isolated. To keep you desperate. To keep you dependent on their charity. Their pity. Their judgment."

He paced as he talked. Made eye contact with individuals. Pulled them in.

"But we know different. We know the truth. We are family. We are chosen. We are free."

More nodding. More agreement. The crowd was with him.

"And when you're family, you take care of each other. You sacrifice for each other. You give everything because you know you'll receive everything in return."

There it was. The setup. The ask hidden in the sermon.

I scanned the crowd, looking for Siobhan. Couldn't see her. Too many people. Too much movement.

Tried to get closer. Stood up, started walking toward the gathering.

Two men noticed. Young. Fit. Not homeless. Not followers. Security dressed as believers.

They moved to intercept me. Casual but deliberate.

"Brother," one said. "First time?"

"Just listening."

"You're welcome here. But maybe stay at the edges. Give the family some space."

Not a request. An order delivered politely.

I stopped walking. Nodded. Backed off.

They watched me until I retreated to my bench. Then turned back to the gathering. Still watching. Still aware.

Cain continued preaching. About surrender. About trust.

About letting go of the old life to embrace the new.

The crowd ate it up.

I'd seen enough. Knew the pattern now. Knew how this worked.

But I needed more. Needed to see Siobhan. Needed to confirm she was here and understand what here meant.

As the gathering broke up, people embracing, laughing, moving in groups toward the encampment areas, I watched for her.

Didn't see her.

But I saw something else.

Cain, surrounded by his inner circle. Talking quietly. Taking an envelope from someone. Counting cash. Giving instructions. The messiah routine dropped for a moment. Just business.

He looked up. Across the crowd. Directly at me.

Eye contact. Recognition. Assessment.

Then a smile. Slight. Knowing.

He'd seen me watching.

And he wanted me to know he'd seen me.

The two security guys started moving my direction again.

I left.

Walked back to my car thinking about that smile. About what it meant.

Saints and sinners look the same from a distance.

Up close, you can tell the difference.

Emmett Cain was no saint.

# Chapter 5: Evening Service

**I came back the next evening.**

Different strategy this time. Dressed down—old jeans, worn flannel shirt, baseball cap. Tried to look like someone seeking instead of someone searching. The distinction mattered.

Parked further away. Walked to the canals from a different direction. Arrived early, before the crowd gathered. Found a spot on the grass near the bridge where I could blend in.

People started arriving around sunset. Same as before. Young and old. Damaged and seeking. They came alone or in pairs, looking for something the world hadn't given them.

I recognized faces from yesterday. A woman in her thirties with matted blonde hair. A kid who couldn't be more than nineteen, neck tattoos and hollow eyes. An older man, maybe sixty, with the dignified bearing of someone who used to be somebody.

They greeted each other like family. Hugs. Smiles. Gentle touches. The physical language of belonging.

More people came. The crowd grew. Forty. Fifty. Sixty.

And then I saw her.

Siobhan Fury.

She walked in with two other young women. Talking, laughing. She looked different from her photo. Thinner, like Kyle said. Hair pulled back. Wearing a loose dress that looked secondhand. But her face—she looked peaceful. Happy in that unsettling way of people who've stopped questioning.

I watched her move through the crowd. She hugged people. Spoke to them with genuine warmth. Seemed fully present. Fully committed.

Not a prisoner. A believer.

That made it harder.

The gathering settled. People found places on the grass. Siobhan sat near the front, cross-legged, attentive. Waiting.

Emmett Cain arrived.

Same entrance as yesterday. Moving through his flock. Touching shoulders. Speaking quiet words. Radiating that dangerous charisma.

He took his position at the center. Stood there for a moment. Let the silence build.

"Family," he said finally.

"Family," they responded. A chorus. A ritual.

"I see you," Cain said.

"We see you," they answered.

The call and response was practiced. Rehearsed. Part of the performance.

"Tonight I want to talk about surrender," Cain began. He had a way of speaking that felt intimate even in a crowd. Like he was talking to each person individually. "The world teaches us to hold on. To grasp. To control. We're told that strength means never letting go. Never admitting we need help. Never showing weakness."

People nodded. Leaned in.

"But that's a lie. The greatest strength is surrender. Admitting we can't do it alone. Opening ourselves to something bigger. To community. To family. To love."

He paced as he spoke. Made eye contact. Drew people in.

"And when we surrender, we become free. Free from ego. Free from fear. Free from the systems that want to keep us small and afraid and alone."

I watched Siobhan. She was transfixed. Drinking in every word.

"But surrender is hard," Cain continued. "It requires trust. It requires giving everything. Your old life. Your old attachments. Your old ideas about who you are. Everything."

There was the edge. The demand hidden in the poetry.

I'd read about this. Elmore Leonard wrote cons better than anyone—the way they make the mark want to be conned. Cain had that gift. Made surrender sound like freedom. Made giving everything sound like getting everything.

"Some of you are still holding on," he said, his voice gentle but firm. "Still keeping one foot in the old world. Still protecting parts of yourself. I understand. I was there once. But I'm here to tell you—you can't be half in. You can't serve two masters. You have to choose."

The pressure was subtle. Wrapped in compassion. But it was pressure nonetheless.

"And when you choose, when you fully surrender, the family provides everything. Food. Shelter. Purpose. Love. We take care of our own. Always."

A young man stood up from the crowd. "How do we show we've surrendered?" he asked. "How do we prove we're worthy?"

Perfect timing. Probably planted.

Cain smiled. "You don't prove anything, brother. Surrender isn't about worthiness. It's about trust. Trust that the family will care for you. And in return, you care for the family. You contribute what you can. Your time. Your skills. Your resources. Not because you have to. Because you want to. Because we're one."

Contribution again. The gentle language of extraction.

"Some of you work," Cain said, his eyes scanning the crowd. "You bring your paychecks to the family. You share your disability checks. Your inheritances. Your gifts from the old world. You do this not because I ask, but because you understand. When everyone gives everything, everyone has everything."

The math didn't work. Never did in these arrangements. But people wanted to believe.

"Others contribute differently," Cain continued. "You help with outreach. You bring new family members. You serve the community in ways that matter. Every contribution is sacred. Every act of giving is an act of love."

I thought about the young women. About Siobhan. About what "serving the community" might actually mean.

The sermon went on for another twenty minutes. More talk of surrender and family and freedom. More gentle pressure disguised as enlightenment. More manipulation wrapped in love.

Then came the testimonials.

People stood and shared their stories. How Cain saved them. How the family gave them purpose. How they'd never felt more whole.

A woman in her forties talked about being homeless for three years before Emmett found her. Now she had shelter. Had hope. Had family.

A young man described his addiction. His recovery through surrender. His gratitude.

Then Siobhan stood.

My stomach tightened.

"I want to thank Prophet Emmett," she said. Her voice was clear. Strong. "Six weeks ago I was lost. My mother had died. I felt like I was drowning in grief and loneliness. I didn't know who I was or why I mattered."

The crowd listened. Attentive. Supportive.

"Then I met Emmett. And he showed me that I wasn't alone. That I was chosen. That I had a family waiting for me. I've surrendered everything—my old apartment, my old job, my old identity. And I've never felt more free."

People applauded. Cain smiled at her with what looked like genuine pride.

"The old world wanted me small," Siobhan continued. "Wanted me to just work and consume and die. But this family wants me whole. Wants me to serve something bigger. To be part of something real."

She sat down. The woman next to her hugged her. Others reached over to touch her shoulder. Affirmation. Reinforcement.

I wanted to grab her. Shake her. Tell her it was all bullshit.

But she wouldn't hear it. Not now. Not like this.

The gathering ended with more embracing. More affirmation. People stood slowly, reluctant to leave the warm circle of belonging.

I stayed seated. Watched Siobhan move with her group toward the encampment area behind Rose Avenue.

Started to follow.

One of Cain's security guys stepped in front of me.

"You were here yesterday," he said.

"Public space," I said. "Free country."

"Just observing? Or looking for something specific?"

I met his eyes. Young guy. Mid-twenties. Military bearing. Not a true believer. Hired help.

"Just listening," I said.

"Emmett noticed you. He wants to know if you're interested in joining the family. If so, we can introduce you properly. If not..." He let it hang.

"If not?"

"Then maybe you should find another place to spend your evenings."

"That a threat?"

"An observation. Like yours."

We stood there. Two men pretending civility while measuring each other for violence.

Finally I stepped back.

"Tell Emmett I'm still thinking about it," I said.

"Tell him yourself. He's always available to those who seek."

The security guy walked away. Back to his post. Still watching.

I headed to my car. Got in. Sat there in the dark.

Thought about Siobhan's testimony. The conviction in her voice. The peace on her face.

She believed every word.

And that was the problem.

You can't save someone who doesn't want saving.

But I'd made a promise to Declan Fury.

Which meant I needed a different approach.

Needed to get inside. Needed to see what was really happening behind the sermons and the testimonials.

Needed to become what I was hunting.

I started the car.

Drove back to Echo Park thinking about surrender.

And what it costs.

# Chapter 6: Torres

**The diner was in Culver City, halfway between her world and mine.**

Late evening. The place was mostly empty. A couple of truckers at the counter. A lone woman in a booth working on a laptop. The smell of coffee and fryer grease and fluorescent exhaustion.

Maria Torres was already there when I arrived. Back booth, facing the door. Old cop habit. She had a cup of coffee in front of her and the look of someone who'd been dealing with bureaucratic bullshit all day.

I slid into the seat across from her.

"Blair," she said.

"Torres."

We'd known each other twelve years. She'd been my rookie partner for six months before I imploded. Before the drinking got too bad and I missed that backup call and nearly got another cop killed. She was one of three people from my police life who still answered when I called.

The waitress came over. Older woman, tired eyes, efficient movements.

"Coffee," I said.

"Food?"

"Just coffee."

She poured, left the pot, walked away.

Torres waited until she was gone. "You sounded stressed on the phone."

"I need information."

"You always need information. That's why you call me."

"This one's different."

"They're always different." She sipped her coffee. Studied me. "You look like shit."

"Three days sober. Well, four now."

"Congratulations. You want a medal or just the information?"

That was Torres. No sentiment. Just reality. One of the things I liked about her.

"Emmett Cain," I said. "Street preacher operating out of Venice Beach. Running some kind of ministry for the homeless population. You know him?"

Her expression changed. Became careful.

"I know the name."

"What do you know?"

"Why are you asking?"

"Missing person case. Young woman named Siobhan Fury. Got involved with Cain's organization about six weeks ago. Stopped contact with family and friends. I found her. She's with him voluntarily. Fully committed."

"So she's not missing. She's where she wants to be."

"She's twenty-three and brainwashed."

"Brainwashed isn't a crime."

"What he's doing to her might be."

Torres leaned back. Looked at me hard. "What exactly do you think he's doing?"

"Don't know yet. But I've watched him operate. Classic cult recruitment. Love bombing. Isolation. Pressure to 'contribute.' Money changing hands. Security that's not security. It smells wrong."

"A lot of things smell wrong. Doesn't make them illegal."

"You investigating him?"

She hesitated. That hesitation told me everything.

"Officially? No."

"Unofficially?"

She glanced around the diner. Making sure no one was listening. Lowered her voice.

"There have been inquiries. Family members looking for missing persons. Young women mostly. All connected to Cain's ministry. All disappeared into his organization voluntarily. No evidence of kidnapping. No evidence of coercion. Just people exercising their right to join a religious community."

"How many inquiries?"

"Seven. In the last two years."

"Jesus."

"Yeah."

"And the department's doing nothing?"

Her jaw tightened. "The department is aware. But there's political pressure. City officials see Cain as helping the homeless crisis. Getting people off the streets. Providing community services. They don't want negative attention on someone who makes their numbers look better."

"Even if he's exploiting them?"

"Exploiting them how? You got evidence of crimes? Trafficking? Abuse? Fraud?"

I didn't. Not yet.

"He's running a con," I said. "I've seen it. The sermons, the pressure to surrender everything, the talk about contribution. He's extracting money and labor from vulnerable people."

"Sounds like every church in America."

"This is different."

"Prove it."

We sat there. The coffee between us getting cold. The fluorescent lights humming overhead.

"What about Vice?" I asked. "Narcotics? Anyone looking at him from those angles?"

"Vice has had eyes on the operation. Suspect there's prostitution involved. Drug dealing using followers as mules. But they can't get close. Cain's careful. Keeps everything just legal enough. Just ambiguous enough."

"So everyone knows he's dirty but no one can touch him."

"Welcome to modern policing." She drank her coffee. "What are you planning to do?"

"Keep looking. Find evidence. Get the girl out."

"And if she doesn't want out?"

"Then I show her father I tried."

Torres nodded. Understood the moral economics of the job.

"There's something else you should know," she said. "I did some digging after you called. Emmett Cain doesn't exist before three years ago. No records. No history. Like he appeared fully formed."

"Fake identity."

"Probably. I ran facial recognition through our database.

Nothing came back. Either he's clean or he's good at staying invisible."

"Can you dig deeper? Real name, criminal history, anything?"

"I can try. But Blair..." She leaned forward. "This is off the books. I'm doing this as a favor. If it blows back on me, if there's an investigation and my name comes up, I've got a daughter to support and a pension to protect."

"I understand."

"Do you? Because you've got nothing to lose. I've got everything."

She was right. I'd already lost my badge, my marriage that never was, my father's respect before he died. Had nothing left except a shitty office and a three-day sobriety streak.

"I won't burn you," I said. "Whatever I find, I'll find it myself. You're just a friend who had coffee with me."

"That better be true."

"It is."

She pulled out her phone. Showed me a photo. Man in his early forties, clean-cut, wearing a suit. Corporate headshot.

"Michael Emmett," she said. "Insurance adjuster from Riverside. Embezzled from his company about four years ago. Investigation was underway when he disappeared. Never charged because they couldn't find him."

I looked at the photo. Same bone structure as Cain. Same eyes. Different presentation.

"That's him."

"Yeah. Changed his name, grew his hair out, became a prophet. Reinvention as survival strategy."

"What else?"

"He had a brother. David Emmett. Arrested on drug charges twelve years ago. Died in county jail. Officially ruled suicide."

Something cold moved through my chest.

"Who arrested him?"

Torres met my eyes. "You did, Blair. You were the arresting officer."

The diner went quiet. Or maybe it was just my head.

"You sure?"

"Checked the arrest record twice. Detective Peter Blair. LAPD. Twelve years ago. The brother, David Emmett, was found hanging in his cell three days after arrest. Inquest ruled it suicide but the family claimed negligence."

I tried to remember. Twelve years ago I was still on the force. Still drinking but hiding it better. Made a lot of arrests back then. A lot of faces. A lot of names.

Couldn't remember David Emmett.

Couldn't remember his brother.

"Does Cain know?" I asked. "That I arrested his brother?"

"Don't know. But if he's smart, and he seems smart, he's done his research on you by now. Private investigators aren't hard to track."

That smile yesterday. The way Cain looked at me. Recognition.

He knew.

Had known all along.

Jim Thompson wrote about people waiting years for revenge. Making it perfect. Making it hurt. Cain had three years to build his operation and wait for me to stumble into it.

"Christ," I said.

"Yeah."

"This changes things."

"How?"

"He's not just running a con. He's got a personal stake. His brother died in custody after I arrested him. That's motive."

"Motive for what?"

"Revenge. Whatever he's planning, I'm part of it."

Torres shook her head. "You're being paranoid. He's running a profitable scam. You're just a PI looking for a missing girl. Why would he care about you?"

"Because I put his brother in the cage where he died."

"His brother put himself there when he broke the law."

Cop logic. Clean and simple. But families don't see it that way.

"I need to be careful," I said.

"You need to walk away. This isn't just a missing person anymore. This is personal. Emotional. You're compromised."

She was right. But walking away wasn't an option.

"I made a promise to her father."

"Fuck the promise. Stay alive."

The waitress came by, topped off our coffee. We sat quiet until she left.

"One more thing," Torres said. "If you're going to keep working this, keep me updated. I can't help officially, but I can watch your back. Unofficially."

"Why would you do that?"

"Because you were a good cop once. And because I owe you."

Old debts. The currency of broken lives.

"The shooting," I said. "Your first year. That's paid off. You don't owe me anything."

"I decide what I owe. Not you." She stood up. Dropped cash on the table for her coffee. "Be careful, Blair. Cain's dangerous. And now you know he's got reasons to hurt you beyond just protecting his operation."

"Noted."

"I mean it. Don't get killed over this girl."

"I'll try."

She left. I sat there with my coffee and the weight of twelve-year-old sins.

Thought about David Emmett. Tried to pull up a memory. A face. Anything.

Nothing came.

Just another arrest in a long line of arrests. Another name in a file somewhere. Another person whose life intersected with mine and ended badly.

I'd been a cop. Done my job. Made arrests. Some of those people went to jail. Some of those people died there.

Not my fault.

But try telling that to their brothers.

I finished my coffee. Left money on the table. Walked out into the Culver City night.

Emmett Cain knew who I was.

Which meant every move I made, he was watching.

And whatever he had planned, I was part of the design.

Time to find out what that design looked like.

Before it closed around me.

# Chapter 7: Night Thoughts

**Couldn't sleep.**

Two a.m. and I was pacing my studio apartment like a caged animal. Which is what I was, basically. Trapped in six hundred square feet of Echo Park desperation.

The Murphy bed was down but I wasn't in it. Just kept moving. Window to kitchen to bathroom to window. Wearing a path in carpet that was already worn through to nothing.

My mind wouldn't stop.

David Emmett. Twelve years ago. County jail. Suicide.

I'd made thousands of arrests. Good arrests, bad arrests, questionable arrests. The kind you make at three a.m. when you're half-drunk and the guy's half-compliant and everything's half-legal. The kind that look fine on paper and feel wrong in your gut.

Couldn't remember this one specifically.

That was the worst part. A man died and I couldn't even remember his face.

I went to my laptop. Sat at the small table that served as desk, dining table, and catchall for my life's paperwork. Opened the computer.

Searched.

David Emmett. Los Angeles. Arrest. 2013.

Found a brief news story. Small article in the Times. Local news section.

*Man Found Dead in County Jail. David Emmett, 31, arrested on drug possession charges, was found hanged in his cell. Sheriff's department investigating. Family claims negligence.*

That was it. Three sentences. A life reduced to a paragraph nobody read.

I searched deeper. Found the arrest record. My name on it. Detective Peter Blair. Possession with intent to distribute. Routine bust based on a tip. Emmett had two priors. Bail set at fifty thousand. He couldn't make it. Three days later, dead.

The family's claim of negligence went nowhere. Inquest ruled it suicide. Case closed. File forgotten.

Except Michael Emmett—now Emmett Cain—hadn't forgotten.

Had spent three years building an operation. Building a persona. Building a trap.

And I'd walked right into it.

Beckett wrote that we're all born astride a grave. The light gleams an instant, then it's night once more. I was starting to understand what he meant. My past kept pulling me down into darkness I'd thought I'd left behind.

I closed the laptop.

Looked at the bottle.

It was sitting on the kitchen counter where it had been sitting for four months. Jameson. Irish whiskey. Three-quarters full. A gift from a client I'd helped find her missing husband. He'd been in Reno with his secretary. Standard issue betrayal. She paid me extra and bought me a bottle as thanks.

I hadn't touched it. Not in four months. Not through the relapses and the meetings and the long nights when sobriety felt like a punishment instead of a prize.

But I was looking at it now.

Four days sober. Longest streak in two months.

The bottle sat there. Patient. Knowing I'd come around eventually.

I stood up. Walked to the kitchen. Picked it up.

Felt the weight of it. The promise of it. The smooth glass cool in my hand.

One drink wouldn't hurt. One drink to stop the thoughts. To quiet the noise. To make David Emmett's ghost stop staring at me with eyes I couldn't remember.

I unscrewed the cap.

Smelled it. Peat and honey and oblivion.

My phone rang.

I looked at the screen. Lonnie. My sponsor. Calling at two in the morning because he had some kind of psychic sobriety alarm that went off whenever I was about to fuck up.

I set the bottle down. Answered.

"Yeah."

"You drinking?" His voice gravelly. Old jazz singer who'd quit everything except coffee and meetings.

"Not yet."

"But thinking about it."

"Yeah."

"Where are you?"

"Home. Holding a bottle. Having a conversation with myself about whether four days is worth protecting."

"It is."

"Easy for you to say. You've got twenty-five years."

"I've got today. Same as you." He paused. I could hear him moving around, probably getting coffee, probably sitting in his Malibu house with the ocean view and the life I'd never have. "What happened?"

I told him. About the case. About Siobhan. About Emmett Cain and his dead brother and the way the past shows up like a bill you forgot to pay.

He listened without interrupting. One of the things that made him a good sponsor. He actually listened.

"So you think this preacher's been waiting for you?" he asked when I finished.

"Maybe. I don't know. Torres thinks I'm paranoid. But that look he gave me... he knows who I am."

"Even if he does, even if this is some elaborate revenge plot, how does drinking help?"

"It doesn't. But it makes me stop thinking about it for a while."

"And when you wake up? When the bottle's empty and the thoughts come back worse than before? What then?"

Same question he always asked. Same answer I never had.

"I don't know, Lonnie."

"You know what I think? I think you're looking for permission. Permission to drink because the situation's hard. Because there's danger. Because you arrested some guy twelve years ago who made bad choices and paid for them. You want me to say it's okay. That you deserve a pass."

"Do I?"

"No. Nobody does. That's not how this works."

I looked at the bottle. Still sitting there. Still patient.

"You can't save everyone, Blair. Can't save the girl if she doesn't want saving. Can't save your career. Can't save the dead. All you can do is not drink today. That's it. That's the whole program."

"Sounds simple when you say it."

"It is simple. Doesn't mean it's easy."

We sat there on the phone. Him in Malibu. Me in Echo Park. Both of us awake in the middle of the night for different reasons.

"You going to drink?" he asked finally.

I screwed the cap back on the bottle. Put it back on the counter.

"Not tonight."

"Good. Call me tomorrow. Let me know you're still vertical."

"Will do."

"And Blair? That girl. Siobhan. You can't carry her and your sobriety. One of them's going to break. Make sure it's not you."

He hung up.

I stood in my kitchen.

Looked at the bottle.

Looked at my apartment.

Looked at my life.

Thought about Declan Fury. About his daughter. About the promise I'd made.

Thought about Emmett Cain. About his brother. About revenge that waits years to ripen.

Thought about me. About who I was and who I'd been and whether there was any difference.

Went to the sink. Poured the bottle down the drain.

Watched twelve-year-old Jameson disappear into LA's sewers where it belonged.

Felt like a grand gesture. Felt like nothing at all.

The bottle was empty but the thirst wasn't.

It never was.

I went back to my laptop. Started planning.

If I was going to get close to Cain, if I was going to find evidence and get Siobhan out, I needed to go all in.

Needed to infiltrate.

Needed to become one of them.

Needed to play the role of lost soul seeking salvation.

Wasn't much of a stretch.

I made notes. Backstory. Motivation. What to say and what to hide. How to seem vulnerable without being weak. How to seem committed without being trapped.

Method acting for a one-man show.

The sun started coming up. Gray light through my window. The city waking up to another day of pretending to care.

I'd gotten through the night. Didn't drink. Didn't sleep either, but you can't have everything.

Made coffee. Strong and black and bitter. The good stuff.

Thought about what Lonnie said. About carrying Siobhan and carrying my sobriety. About one of them breaking.

He was probably right.

But I'd made a promise to Declan.

And unlike the bottle, promises were something I tried to keep.

Even the ones that would kill me.

I showered. Shaved. Put on my worst clothes. Looked at myself in the mirror.

Saw exactly what I needed to see.
A man with nothing left to lose.
Perfect.

# Chapter 8: Undercover

**I looked homeless.**

Wasn't hard. Just stopped trying not to.

Wore jeans I'd had for ten years. flannel shirt with a rip in the sleeve. Work boots that had seen better decades. Didn't shave. Didn't shower. Let myself get that particular look of someone who'd stopped caring about appearances because appearances stopped mattering.

Drove to Venice mid-morning. Parked the Honda six blocks away in a neighborhood where it wouldn't get towed. Walked to the beach carrying nothing but myself and a backstory I'd rehearsed all night.

The encampment behind Rose Avenue was bigger in daylight. Fifty tents at least. Tarps and shopping carts and the infrastructure of displacement. People moving through their routines. Making coffee on camp stoves. Sorting through donated clothes. Having conversations that looked normal if you ignored the context.

I didn't walk straight in. Hung around the edges. Sat on a bench near the basketball courts. Watched. Waited.

George V. Higgins wrote that criminals are just people doing a job. Same with the homeless. Same with everyone. We're all just trying to get through the day without it killing us.

After an hour, a young woman approached me.

Early twenties. Brown hair pulled back. Bright eyes that had seen too much but still held hope. She carried a backpack and that particular energy of someone on a mission.

"Hey," she said. "You okay?"

"Been better."

"You need anything? Water? Food?"

"I'm alright."

She sat down next to me. Not too close. Respectful of space.

"I'm Rachel. I volunteer with a community here. We help people. No judgment. No strings."

The pitch. Delivered with genuine warmth.

"What kind of community?" I asked.

"People who care about each other. Who look out for one another. Family, basically." She smiled. "You look like you could use some family."

"Don't we all."

"You have a place to stay?"

"Here and there."

"How long you been on the street?"

I'd prepared for this. Had a story ready. Mix of truth and fiction. Easier to remember that way.

"Few months. Had an apartment in Echo Park. Lost my job. Couldn't make rent. The rest is the usual story."

"What did you do? Before."

"Security work mostly. Private stuff. But I've got a record. Makes it hard to get hired."

"What kind of record?"

"DUI. Assault. The kind of mistakes you make when you're drinking too much and caring too little."

All true. Just rearranged to fit the narrative.

Rachel nodded.

No judgment in her eyes. Just acceptance.

"A lot of us have records. A lot of us made mistakes. That's why we're here. Prophet Emmett says the past doesn't define us. Only our choices now matter."

"Prophet Emmett."

"He runs our community. He's amazing. Really sees people. Helps them find purpose again."

"Sounds too good to be true."

"I thought so too at first. But it's real. I've been with the family six months. Changed my life."

She had that glow. That certainty. The look of someone who'd found meaning and wanted to share it.

"You hungry?" she asked.

"I could eat."

"Come on. We're serving lunch in an hour. You can meet some people. See what we're about. No pressure."

I followed her into the encampment.

People looked up as we passed. Some nodded. Some ignored us. The same social dynamics as anywhere else. Just played out in tents instead of houses.

Rachel led me to a larger tent structure. Inside, a dozen people were preparing food. Big pots of soup. Sandwiches being assembled. Bottles of water in coolers.

"Everyone," Rachel called out. "This is... I'm sorry, I didn't get your name."

"Peter," I said. Then caught myself. "But people call me Pete."

"Pete's new. Thought we could show him some hospitality."

The group welcomed me. Genuine smiles. Handshakes. Names I tried to remember.

There was Marcus, older Black man with kind eyes and gray beard. Sarah, young woman covered in tattoos. Jason, kid who couldn't be more than twenty. Others whose names blurred together.

They put me to work making sandwiches. Peanut butter and jelly. The universal food of limited resources.

We worked and talked. They asked questions but didn't pry. Shared their own stories freely. Marcus had been an electrician before his wife died and he couldn't keep it together. Sarah was running from an abusive ex. Jason aged out of foster care with nowhere to go.

All of them talked about Emmett like he'd saved them.

"He gave me hope," Marcus said. "When I had nothing, he gave me family."

"He sees the real you," Sarah added. "Not what the world says about you. What you actually are."

"He's the real deal," Jason said. "Not like those other preachers who want your money and give you nothing. Emmett actually cares."

I listened. Nodded. Played the role of interested skeptic becoming believer.

After an hour of prep, people started arriving for lunch. Homeless folks from the encampment. Some from the family. Others just passing through looking for a meal.

We served them. Handed out soup and sandwiches and water. No sermons. No conditions. Just food.

It felt legitimate. Felt real.

Which was the genius of it. Hide the con inside actual good works.

Emmett Cain appeared around one p.m.

He moved through the lunch service like a politician working a crowd. Stopped at each person. Made eye contact. Asked questions. Remembered names. The full charisma treatment.

When he got to me, he stopped.

"New face," he said.

"Pete," I said. Extended my hand.

He shook it. Firm grip. Warm smile. Eyes that looked right through you.

"Welcome, Pete. Rachel bring you in?"

"Yeah. She's been kind."

"She's good at that. We all are. It's what family does." He studied me. "You look familiar. Have we met?"

My heart rate picked up. Kept my expression neutral.

"Don't think so. I've got one of those faces."

"Maybe." He didn't look convinced. "Where you from?"

"Originally? All over. Lately, Echo Park."

"What brought you to Venice?"

"Heard there was community here. Figured I'd check it out."

"And what do you think so far?"

"Seems real. That's rare."

He smiled. Approved of the answer.

"It is real. Because we make it real. Every day. Together." He put his hand on my shoulder. "Stay for the evening service tonight. You'll understand better then."

"I might do that."

"I hope you do. We can always use another brother."

He moved on. Worked the rest of the crowd. But I felt his attention still on me. That awareness.

He knew.

Or suspected.

Or was playing a game I didn't understand yet.

Rachel came over after he'd left.

"He talked to you! That's amazing. He doesn't always do that with new people."

"He seems genuine."

"He is. You'll see. The more time you spend here, the more you'll understand. This isn't just a meal program. It's a whole new way of living."

"What's the catch?"

"No catch. Just commitment. To the family. To each other. To something bigger than yourself."

There it was. The gentle pressure disguised as invitation.

We finished serving lunch. Cleaned up. Rachel invited me to stay, hang around, be part of the afternoon activities.

I did.

Spent the next few hours embedded in the community. Helped with various tasks. Talked to people. Learned the rhythms.

Watched for Siobhan. Didn't see her.

Watched for the darker elements. The exploitation. The control.

Saw only kindness and community and people helping each other.

Which made it harder.

Because I knew it was there. Underneath the good works. The con within the charity.

I just had to wait long enough to see it.

Evening service was at dusk. Same as before. The gathering by the bridge.

I went. Sat with Rachel and her group. Listened to Emmett preach about surrender and family and finding your purpose.

Watched people respond.

Watched them believe.

Watched Siobhan enter late and sit near the front. She looked healthy. Happy. Committed.

During the testimonials, a young man stood up and talked about how he'd signed over his disability check to the family. How he'd never felt freer.

The crowd applauded.

I understood the mechanism now. Public testimony as peer pressure. Display your loyalty. Prove your commitment. Show others what's expected.

Classic cult psychology.

After the service, Rachel introduced me to more people. I met a dozen members of the inner circle. They were welcoming. Warm. Insisted I come back tomorrow.

Emmett found me before I could leave.

"Pete," he said. "Walk with me a moment."

We walked away from the crowd. Toward the canal bridge. Just the two of us.

"You seem different from most people who come here," he said.

"How so?"

"More watchful. More careful. Like you're assessing rather than experiencing."

"Old habits. I used to work security."

"Right. You mentioned that." He stopped. Looked at me directly. "I want you to know something. This community is built on trust. On honesty. On people being real with each other. If you're here for the wrong reasons, it won't work. The family knows. We always know."

"I'm just looking for somewhere to belong."

"Are you? Or are you looking for something else?"

We stood there. Two men playing chess with words.

"I'm looking for what everyone's looking for," I said finally. "Meaning. Purpose. Connection."

"And you think you'll find it here?"

"Maybe. Too soon to tell."

He smiled. "Fair enough. Take your time. Figure it out. But know this: we protect our family. Fiercely. Anyone who threatens it, anyone who tries to harm it, we deal with them."

Not a threat. Just information.

"Understood," I said.

"Good." He extended his hand again. "I hope you join us, Pete. I really do. You seem like someone who needs what we're offering."

I shook his hand.

Felt the weight of his attention.

Felt the danger.

We parted. I walked back toward where I'd parked the Honda. Six blocks through Venice in the dark.

Thought about what I'd learned. About what I'd seen. About how deep I'd have to go to get what I needed.

Thought about Emmett's warning.

He was on to me.

Or testing me.

Or both.
Either way, I was in it now.
No turning back.

# Chapter 9: The Family Meal

**I came back the next evening.**

Rachel had texted me. Which meant I'd given her my number. Which meant I was officially on their radar. The phone was burner, prepaid, nothing connected to Peter Blair PI. But still. I was in the system now.

The text said: *Family dinner tonight 6pm. Would love to see you there.*

Love. Always love with these people. The word worn smooth from overuse.

I showed up at six. Same clothes. Same rough appearance. Playing the part.

The dinner was in a different location. An actual house near the canals. Two-story, needed paint, probably worth two million dollars because Venice real estate had lost its mind. The kind of place that looked run-down but sat on land that cost more than most people made in a lifetime.

Rachel met me at the door.

"Pete! You came!" Genuine happiness. She hugged me. I stiffened, then returned it awkwardly. Physical affection wasn't my default.

"Said I would."

"Come in. Everyone's excited to meet you properly."

Inside, the house was crowded. Thirty, forty people. The smell of cooking food. Laughter. Conversations overlapping. It looked like any dinner party. Felt like something else.

The furniture was minimal. Goodwill quality. But the space was clean. Organized. Photos on the walls of the family at various gatherings. Emmett in the center of most of them. Arms around people. Smiling that warm, charismatic smile.

Rachel led me through the crowd. Introduced me to more people than I could remember. Everyone welcoming. Everyone asking the same questions. Where you from. How'd you find us. What do you need.

I gave the same answers. Built the legend. Pete from Echo Park. Lost job. Lost apartment. Looking for community.

They ate it up.

"Dinner's almost ready," Rachel said. "We eat together. Everyone. It's important. Emmett says shared meals build shared bonds."

"Makes sense."

We moved to the back of the house. Large room, probably used to be a living room. Now it was empty except for a long table made of plywood and sawhorses. Mismatched chairs around it. Place settings that didn't match. The aesthetic of poverty but the feeling of intentional community.

People started sitting. I hung back, unsure where to go.

"Pete." A voice behind me.

I turned. Emmett Cain. Dressed simply. Jeans and a button-down shirt. Barefoot. The casual guru look.

"Emmett."

"Glad you came back. Means you're serious about this."

"Still figuring it out."

"Fair. But tonight, just be present. Experience it. Don't analyze. Don't judge. Just be."

Easy for him to say.

He gestured to the table. "Sit anywhere. We don't have hierarchy here. We're all equal."

Bullshit. Every organization has hierarchy. But I nodded and found a seat.

Rachel sat on one side of me. A guy named David on the other. Mid-twenties, earnest face, talked about how Emmett saved him from heroin addiction.

The room filled. People finding seats. Squeezing in.

The energy was good. Positive. Like a real family gathering.

Then Siobhan walked in.

She was with two other women. Laughing at something one of them said.

Her face was open. Relaxed. She looked healthier than in her photo. Fuller. More present.

She sat across the table from me. Two seats down.

Close enough to see. Far enough to not be obvious.

Our eyes met for a second.

No recognition.

I was just another face in her new family.

Emmett stood at the head of the table. Raised his hands. The room went quiet.

"Family," he said.

"Family," everyone responded.

"Before we eat, let's take a moment. Hold hands with the people next to you."

The table joined hands. Rachel's hand was small and warm. David's was calloused and strong. I felt uncomfortable. Exposed. But I held on.

"Close your eyes," Emmett said. "Breathe. Feel the connection. We are one body. One heart. One purpose."

The room breathed together. I kept my eyes open. Watched. Watched Emmett watching his flock. The satisfaction on his face.

"We're grateful," he continued. "For this food. For this family. For this moment. We're grateful for those who contributed. Who sacrificed. Who gave so that all could receive. This is love in action."

People murmured agreement.

"Open your eyes. Let's eat."

The meal began. Platters of food passed around. Simple stuff. Rice. Beans. Chicken. Salad. Someone had cooked for forty people on a tight budget and made it work.

Conversation flowed. People talked and laughed and shared stories. I listened more than I spoke. Gathered information.

Learned that most of the people here didn't live in the house. They lived in the encampments. In tents. In cars. This was just a gathering space. A communal center.

But some lived here. The inner circle. The trusted ones.

Siobhan was one of them.

I watched her interact. She was comfortable. Confident. Passed food. Made jokes. Touched people's shoulders as she talked. The body language of belonging.

"She's amazing, right?" David said next to me.

"Who?"

"Siobhan. The woman you keep looking at." He smiled. No judgment. Just observation. "She joined a couple months ago. One of Emmett's favorites. Really embraced the teachings."

"What teachings?"

"Surrender. Service. Community over self. The things that matter."

Tom Waits sang about people selling their souls for a song. Sometimes they did it for less. For a meal. For a smile. For the illusion of family.

"How long have you been here?" I asked David.

"Eight months. Best eight months of my life. I was dying before this. Literally. Using every day. Living under a bridge. Hating myself. Then Rachel found me. Brought me here. Emmett talked to me for three hours that first night. Really listened. Saw me. Gave me hope."

"And now?"

"Now I'm clean. I'm useful. I'm part of something bigger. I work for the family. We all do. Whatever we can contribute."

"What do you contribute?"

"Outreach mostly. Finding people who need help. Bringing them in. Sometimes I do runs for Emmett. Deliveries and stuff. Whatever's needed."

Deliveries. The word hung there.

"What kind of deliveries?"

He looked at me. Something shifted in his eyes. Caution.

"Just family business. Supplies. Donations. That kind of thing."

He was lying. Or half-lying. The way people do when they know the truth is ugly but want to believe it's not.

"Cool," I said. Backed off.

The meal continued. Dessert came out. Store-bought cake. People sang happy birthday to someone. A woman in her fifties who looked like life had beaten her down but was trying to get back up.

She cried during the song. Happy tears.

After dinner, people cleared plates. Washed dishes. The communal cleanup.

I helped. Carried plates to the kitchen. Washed alongside others.

Siobhan was drying.

We stood next to each other at the sink. Close enough to talk.

"You're new," she said.

"Yeah. Pete."

"Siobhan." She smiled. Handed me a wet plate to wash. "What brought you here?"

"Looking for community. Rachel invited me."

"She's good at that. Finding people who need us."

"You been here long?"

"Couple months. Feels like forever though. In a good way. Like I finally found where I'm supposed to be."

"That's good."

"Where are you staying?" she asked.

"Here and there. The encampment mostly."

"You should talk to Emmett about staying in the house. There's room. If you're committed."

"Maybe."

We worked in silence for a moment. Plates passing between us. The mundane intimacy of shared tasks.

"Can I ask you something?" she said.

"Sure."

"Do you believe in purpose? Like real purpose. Not just going through the motions but actually mattering."

"I don't know. Maybe."

"I didn't either. Before this. I thought life was just random. You're born. You suffer. You die. But Emmett showed me different. Showed me we're all connected. We all matter. We just have to surrender to it."

Her eyes were bright. Certain. The look of someone who'd found religion and wanted to convert you.

"My mom died," she continued. "Two years ago. I thought I'd never stop hurting. Never find meaning again. But here... here I found family. Found purpose. Found peace."

I wanted to grab her. Shake her. Tell her it was all a con. Tell her Emmett was using her. Tell her to call her father who was paying me five hundred dollars he couldn't afford to find her.

Instead I said, "That's good. I'm glad you found it."

"You will too. If you stay. If you open yourself to it."

We finished the dishes.

The evening wound down. People started leaving. Hugs at the door. Promises to see each other tomorrow.

Emmett found me before I left.

"Walk with me," he said. Not a request.

We went outside. Walked along the canal. The water was still and dark. Reflected the lights from the million-dollar houses.

"What did you think of tonight?" he asked.

"Seemed genuine."

"It is genuine. That's what people don't understand. They think community has to be fake. Has to be hiding something. But sometimes people just caring for each other is exactly what it looks like."

"Sometimes."

He stopped. Looked at me.

"You're still skeptical. I can feel it. You're watching instead of participating. Analyzing instead of experiencing."

"Old habits."

"Or current purposes." His voice shifted. Harder. "I'm going to be direct with you, Pete. Because I think you can handle it. You're not what you seem. I don't know what you are exactly. But you're not a lost soul looking for community."

My pulse quickened. Kept my face neutral.

"What am I then?"

"That's what I'm trying to figure out. Are you a cop? A reporter? Someone's family member looking for a lost sheep?"

"I'm just a guy who lost his way."

"Maybe. Or maybe you're something else. Either way, I want you to understand something. This family is real. These people matter. And I protect them. From everyone. Including people who lie about who they are."

We stood there. The threat clear now. No more pretense.

"I'm not here to hurt anyone," I said.

"Good. Then we won't have a problem." He smiled. Back to the warm guru persona. "But if you are here for the wrong reasons, you should leave. Before things get complicated. Before people get hurt. Before you do something you'll regret."

He walked away. Left me standing by the canal.

I'd been made.

Not completely. But enough.

He knew I was lying. Just didn't know about what.

I walked back to my car. Got in. Sat there.

Thought about Siobhan. About how deep she was. About how little she suspected.

Thought about Emmett's warning.

Thought about how much time I had before the whole thing collapsed.

Not much.

I needed to move faster. Needed to find evidence. Needed to get her out.

Before Emmett decided I was too much of a threat to tolerate.

Started the engine.

Drove back to Echo Park.

Thinking about family dinners and broken people and the lies we tell ourselves to survive.

Thinking about how close I was to the truth.

And how dangerous close could be.

# Chapter 10: The Prophet Notices

**The text came at midnight.**

*Come to the house tomorrow. 10am. Just you. -E*

I stared at the message. Emmett had my number. Which meant he'd gotten it from Rachel. Which meant the walls were closing.

Didn't respond. Just lay in bed thinking about what tomorrow meant.

A private meeting. One-on-one. Either he was going to expose me or recruit me deeper. Maybe both.

I thought about not going. About calling the whole thing off. Telling Declan I tried and failed. Take what was left of his five hundred dollars and walk away.

But Siobhan's face kept appearing in my mind. The way she looked at dinner. Happy. Committed. Lost.

I'd go.

See what Emmett wanted.

Hope I walked back out.

Morning came too fast. I drove to Venice with coffee and a bad feeling.

The house looked different in daylight. More run-down. More obviously a squat pretending to be a commune.

The door was open. I knocked anyway.

"Come in, Pete." Emmett's voice from inside.

I entered. The house was empty except for him. He sat at the plywood table. Two cups of coffee waiting. Steam rising.

"Sit," he said.

I sat across from him. Didn't touch the coffee.

"You don't trust me," he observed.

"Don't know you well enough to trust you."

"Fair." He sipped his coffee. Watched me over the rim. "But I know you. Better than you think."

"How's that?"

"I make it my business to know people. Especially people who come into my family asking questions."

"I haven't asked questions."

"You don't have to. The way you watch. The way you listen. The way you hold yourself apart. You're not here to join us. You're here to investigate us."

No point denying it now.

"What gave me away?"

"Everything. Your story's too clean. Your desperation too performed. Real broken people have jagged edges. You're smooth. Controlled. Like someone playing a part."

He was good. Better than I'd given him credit for.

"So why am I here?" I asked.

"Because I want to understand what you want. And because I want to give you a choice."

"What choice?"

He leaned back. Relaxed. In control.

"You're looking for someone. The girl. Siobhan. I saw you watching her last night."

My stomach tightened.

"Her father hired you," Emmett continued. "Declan Fury. Former punk rocker. Eight years sober. Desperate to save his daughter from the cult he thinks she's joined."

He'd done his homework. Knew exactly who I was and why I was here.

"She doesn't need saving," he said. "She's exactly where she wants to be. Happy. Purposeful. Part of something bigger than herself."

"She's brainwashed."

"She's awake. For the first time in her life." He drank more coffee. "But I understand. You made a promise to her father. You're trying to honor it. I respect that. Loyalty's rare."

"So what now?"

"Now you have a choice. Walk away. Tell Declan you couldn't find her. Or tell him you found her and she's fine and wants to be left alone. Either way, you leave us in peace."

"And if I don't?"

"Then things get complicated. For you. For her. For everyone."

The threat was clear. But something else was there too. Underneath the words.

"You want me to walk away," I said. "Why not just make me? You've got people. Resources. Could make me disappear if you wanted."

He smiled. "I could. But that creates problems. Missing PI. Police investigation. Attention we don't need. Better if you just leave voluntarily."

"Because you're running something here. Something you don't want investigated."

"I'm running a community. Helping people the system abandoned. That's all."

"The deliveries David mentioned. The contributions you extract. The way you isolate people from their families. That's not help. That's exploitation."

His expression didn't change. But his eyes went cold.

"You don't understand what we do here. What these people need. The world chews them up and spits them out. Tells them they're worthless. We give them value. Give them purpose. Yes, they contribute. Because that's what communities do. Everyone gives what they can. Everyone receives what they need."

"Sounds like communism."

"Sounds like family."

We sat there. Two men on opposite sides of a line neither wanted to cross.

"I knew your brother," I said. "David Emmett."

His whole body went still.

"Did you now."

"Arrested him twelve years ago. Drug charges. He died in county jail three days later. Ruled suicide."

"I know how my brother died." His voice flat. Controlled. "I also know who put him there."

"He put himself there. I just did my job."

"Your job." He laughed. No humor in it. "You arrested him on bullshit charges. Planted evidence. Everyone knew it. But the system protected you because that's what the system does."

"That's not what happened."

"You don't even remember him, do you? Don't remember his face. His name. The way he cried when you cuffed him. You processed him like paperwork. Then went home and forgot he existed."

He was right. I didn't remember. And that made it worse.

"He was my little brother," Emmett said. His voice quiet now. Dangerous. "Smart kid. Funny. Had his whole life ahead of him. Then you arrested him on some bullshit tip from a snitch who wanted to save himself. David couldn't make bail. Sat in that cell for three days. Terrified. Alone. Then hanged himself with a bedsheet."

"I'm sorry."

"Sorry." He stood up. Paced. "You're sorry. That fixes it then. That brings him back."

"No. It doesn't. But I didn't kill him. The system did. The circumstances did. His choices did."

"His choices." Emmett stopped pacing. Looked at me. "You want to talk about choices? Let's talk about yours. You chose to be a cop. Chose to make that arrest. Chose to not give a shit what happened after. Those were your choices. And they killed my brother."

James Ellroy wrote that all cops are damaged. All criminals are damaged. We're all just choosing which side of the law to stand on while we bleed. Emmett and I were bleeding from the same wound, just blaming different people.

"So this is revenge," I said. "The whole operation. You built it waiting for me to show up."

"No. I built it because the world killed my brother and I decided to save people the world wants dead. But when I saw you at that gathering... yeah. That was fate. The universe giving me a gift."

"What gift?"

"The chance to make you understand. Make you feel what I felt. Watching someone you care about get swallowed by a system you can't fight."

"Siobhan."

"She's not in danger from me. She's thriving here. But you caring about her, wanting to save her, not being able to... that's poetry. That's justice."

"You're using her to hurt me."

"I'm giving her the family she needs. What you see as using, I see as healing. But yes, if your pain is a side effect, I'll take it."

He sat back down. Calm again. In control.

"Here's what happens next," he said. "You walk away. Tell Declan his daughter is fine. Tell him she doesn't want to be found. And you leave us alone."

"And if I don't?"

"Then I make sure Siobhan knows who you are. Who sent you. What you did to my brother. I make sure she understands that the man trying to save her is the same man who destroyed her new family's prophet. She already loves me. Already trusts me. You think she'll choose you over me?"

He was right. She wouldn't.

"You're a piece of shit," I said.

"Maybe. But I'm a piece of shit who helps people. What are you?"

Good question.

"I'll think about it," I said.

"Don't think too long. My patience has limits. And if you push me, if you threaten what I've built here, I'll do more than just expose you to Siobhan. I'll make you disappear. Properly this time. No body. No investigation. Just another lost soul who fell through the cracks in Venice Beach."

He stood. Went to the door. Opened it.

"Thanks for the coffee," he said. "Next time bring a better story. Or don't come at all."

I walked out. Got in my car. Drove three blocks before I had to pull over.

Sat there shaking.

Not from fear. From rage.

He'd played me. Used my guilt about his brother. Used my need to save Siobhan. Used everything against me.

And I couldn't do shit about it.

If I pushed harder, he'd turn Siobhan against me. If I backed off, she stayed trapped. If I went to the cops, Torres had already said they couldn't touch him.

I was in a box. And Emmett had built it perfectly.

My phone rang. Declan.

I didn't answer.

Couldn't tell him what I'd learned. Couldn't tell him his daughter was fine and didn't want saving. Couldn't tell him I'd failed.

Not yet.

The phone stopped ringing. Started again.

I answered.

"Blair." His voice rough with hope and fear. "Did you find her?"

"Yeah. I found her."

"Is she okay?"

I looked out at Venice. The palm trees. The sun. The beautiful surface hiding all the rot.

"She's alive," I said. "She's with Emmett Cain's group. She seems... she seems happy."

"Happy? Jesus Christ. What does that mean?"

"Means she's fully committed. Believes in what he's selling. I talked to her. She doesn't want to leave."

Silence on the line. Then: "But she's in danger, right? He's hurting her?"

"I don't know yet. I'm working on it."

"Working on it? I hired you to get her out."

"I know. But it's complicated. She's an adult. She's there voluntarily. I can't just grab her."

"Then what can you do?"

"I'm trying to find evidence. Something to prove he's running a criminal operation. Something to make her see the truth."

"How long will that take?"

"I don't know."

Another silence. Longer this time.

"I'm running out of money, Blair. I gave you everything I had. I need my daughter back."

"I understand."

"Do you? Do you understand what it's like to lose your kid? To know they're out there somewhere being hurt and you can't do anything about it?"

I thought about Emmett. About his brother. About loss and blame and the ways we eat ourselves alive.

"Yeah," I said. "I think I do."

"Then get her out. Please. Whatever it takes."

He hung up.

I sat in my car.

Thought about Emmett's offer. Walk away. Leave Siobhan in her delusion. Take the easy path.

Thought about my promise to Declan.

Thought about David Emmett dying in a cell because of an arrest I couldn't remember.

Started the engine.

Drove back to Echo Park.

I wasn't walking away.

Even if it killed me.

Which it might.

# Chapter 11: Nightwatch

**I needed evidence.**

Not suspicions. Not observations. Hard evidence that Emmett was running something criminal. Something that would make Siobhan see the truth. Something that would give Torres enough to move.

Which meant going deeper.

I showed up at the encampment late afternoon. Found Rachel distributing supplies.

"Pete! Haven't seen you in a couple days."

"Been thinking. About what Emmett said. About commitment."

Her face lit up. "And?"

"I want to try. Really try. Be part of the family."

"That's wonderful!" She hugged me. I was getting used to the constant physical affection. Didn't mean I liked it. "What changed your mind?"

"Talked to Emmett. He made sense. About community. About purpose. Figured I'd stop watching and start participating."

"He has that effect on people. Cuts through the bullshit. Shows you what matters."

"Yeah. Listen, I was wondering. Is there a way to stay here? In the encampment? Really be part of things instead of just visiting?"

She thought about it. "There's space in some of the tents. We share. Nobody has their own space. That's part of it. Communal living."

"I can do that."

"Let me talk to some people. See if there's room."

She walked off. I waited. Watched the encampment activity. People coming and going. The constant movement of survival and community mixed together.

Thirty minutes later, Rachel came back with a guy I'd met before. Marcus. The older man who used to be an electrician.

"Marcus has space in his tent," Rachel said. "If you don't mind tight quarters."

"Don't mind at all."

Marcus nodded. "Welcome, brother. It's not much, but it's dry and safe."

I followed him through the encampment. Past tents and tarps and shopping carts. Past people living their lives in public because they had no private space left.

His tent was near the back. Eight-by-ten, canvas, the kind you'd take camping if camping wasn't your whole life. Inside was surprisingly organized. Sleeping bags. A few crates for storage. Battery-powered lantern. The efficiency of limited space.

"You can have that side," Marcus said, pointing. "I'm up early, so I'll try not to wake you. But no promises."

"I appreciate this."

"We take care of each other. That's the point."

I set down my backpack. The few things I'd brought. Change of clothes. Toothbrush. The basics.

"How long you been here?" I asked.

"Eight months. Since my wife died. Lost the house. Lost everything. Was sleeping rough until the family found me."

"You like it? Living like this?"

He smiled. Sad smile. "Like it? No. But it beats the alternative. And I've got hope now. Emmett says we're building toward something. A real compound. Space for everyone. Just need more resources."

"Resources meaning money."

"And labor. And commitment. Everyone gives what they can. I do electrical work for the family. Help with the house. Whatever's needed."

"What about the others? What do they contribute?"

"Depends. Some work regular jobs, turn over their paychecks. Some get disability, share that. Some help with outreach. Some..." He trailed off.

"Some what?"

"Some do special work. For Emmett. Things that need discretion."

There it was again. The hint of something darker.

"What kind of special work?"

Marcus looked uncomfortable. "Not my business. Not yours either. Point is, everyone serves the family however they can. That's all you need to know."

I let it drop. Didn't want to push too hard.

We spent the evening together. Shared dinner at the communal meal. I met more people. Learned more names. Built more cover.

Siobhan wasn't there. Someone said she was at the house. Working on something for Emmett.

Night fell. The encampment got quiet. People settling into tents. Battery lanterns dimming. The sounds of sleep and discomfort and people making do.

Marcus was out by ten. Snoring softly. The sleep of the exhausted.

I lay there. Waited. Listening.

Around midnight, I heard movement outside. Quiet. Deliberate. Not the random sounds of someone getting up to piss. This was purposeful.

I unzipped the tent quietly. Looked out.

Three figures moving through the encampment. Young people. Two women, one man. Carrying backpacks. Heading toward the street.

I watched them disappear into the darkness.

Waited five minutes. Then followed.

Kept my distance. Stayed in shadows. Old cop skills coming back.

They walked three blocks. Met a car. Black sedan. Tinted windows.

The car door opened. They got in. Not all the way. Just leaned in. Talking to someone inside.

One of the women handed over a backpack. Received an envelope in return.

The exchange took thirty seconds. Then they walked away. The car drove off.

I memorized the license plate. Watched them return to the encampment.

Drug run. Had to be.

Followers used as mules. Pick up product, deliver to dealers, bring back cash.

It was something. Not enough yet. But something.

I went back to Marcus's tent. Settled in. Pretended to sleep.

An hour later, more movement.

This time it was a truck. Pulling up to the edge of the encampment. Two of Emmett's security guys getting out.

They went to one of the larger tents. Knocked. A young woman emerged. Early twenties. I'd seen her at the family dinner.

They talked quietly. She looked scared. But she went with them.

Got in the truck. Drove away.

I wanted to follow. But I was on foot. No way to track them.

Waited to see if she came back.

She did. Three hours later. Same truck. She got out. Walked back to her tent. Her clothes were different. She looked shaken.

Prostitution. The "special work" Marcus had mentioned.

Young women sent out to service clients. Bring back money for the family.

All wrapped in the language of contribution and service.

I felt sick.

Lay there thinking about Siobhan. Wondering if she'd been part of this. If she knew. If she'd convinced herself it was holy somehow.

Raymond Chandler wrote that the streets were dark with something more than night. He meant evil. The casual, organized kind. The kind that wears a friendly face and calls itself family.

Morning came slow.

Marcus woke up. Stretched. Smiled at me.

"Sleep okay?"

"Fine," I lied.

"Good. We've got service this morning. Then work detail. You'll get the rhythm of it."

I went through the motions. Attended the service. Watched Emmett preach. Watched Siobhan sit in the front row, devoted and serene.

Wondered if she knew. If she was part of it.

Wondered how deep I'd have to go to find out.

After the service, Emmett found me.

"Pete. Hear you're staying with us now."

"Trying it out."

"Good. Commitment's important. Can't halfway belong to a family." He put his hand on my shoulder. "Marcus says you're curious about how we operate. About how people contribute."

"Just trying to understand."

"I appreciate that. Tell you what. Come by the house later. I'll show you the whole operation. Transparency's important to us."

It was a test. I knew it. He knew I knew it.

"Okay," I said.

"Four o'clock. Come alone."

He walked away.

I spent the rest of the day in the encampment. Helping with tasks. Building credibility. Watching.

Saw two more late-night runners preparing their backpacks. Saw another young woman being prepped by Rachel, dressed up, told she was doing important work for the family.

Saw the machinery of exploitation dressed up as community service.

At four, I went to the house.

Emmett was waiting. Along with his two main security guys. The ones I'd seen doing the pickups.

"Pete. Come in. Let me show you what we've built here."

He led me through the house. Showed me the communal spaces. The kitchen. The sleeping areas.

Then the basement.

Down narrow stairs. Into a space that was more organized than the rest of the house. Filing cabinets. A desk with a computer. Stacks of cash in a safe that wasn't quite closed.

"This is command center," Emmett said. "Where we coordinate everything. Outreach. Donations. Services."

"Services."

"We help the community in multiple ways. Food. Shelter. Employment opportunities for those who want them."

"Employment like deliveries."

"Among other things. Some of our family members work traditional jobs. Others work for us directly. We find what suits each person's skills and situation."

"And the young women who go out at night?"

His expression didn't change. "Providing companionship to lonely people. It's a service industry. Same as any other. They choose to participate. They get compensated. Everyone wins."

"They're prostitutes."

"They're adults making choices. We don't force anyone. We just provide opportunities."

"Wrapped in religious rhetoric about serving the family."

"You say rhetoric. I say framework. People need meaning. We give them meaning along with opportunity. What's wrong with that?"

Everything. But I kept my face neutral.

"And the drug deliveries?"

"Medication distribution. Some of our donors prefer alternative treatments. We facilitate that. It's all consensual. All adult choices."

He was good. Had an answer for everything. Framed exploitation as empowerment.

"Here's the thing, Pete. Or should I call you Peter? Peter Blair, private investigator, former LAPD, currently working for Declan Fury to extract his daughter from my terrible cult."

The security guys moved closer.

"You've seen what you wanted to see," Emmett continued. "Spent the night. Watched the operation. Gathered your evidence. Now what?"

"Now I tell Siobhan the truth. Show her what you're really doing."

"Go ahead. Tell her. She'll choose me over you. Every time. Because I give her something you can't. Purpose. Family. Love. Your truth is just words. Mine is lived experience."

He was right and we both knew it.

"But I'll make you a deal," he said. "Since you're so concerned about Siobhan. Since you care so much about saving her from the terrible fate of being happy and purposeful. I'll let her go. Free and clear. On one condition."

"What condition?"

"You take her place."

I stared at him.

"Join us. Really join us. Work for the family. Make deliveries. Do the hard work. Contribute everything like everyone else. Do that, and I'll release Siobhan. Send her home to daddy with my blessing."

"Why would you do that?"

"Because watching you degrade yourself to save her? Watching you become what you judge? That's worth more to me than keeping one girl. That's poetry. That's justice for my brother."

The room went quiet.

"You're serious."

"Completely. Stay for a month. Do whatever I tell you. Prove you're willing to sacrifice for her the way she's sacrificed for us. Then she walks. And you walk. And we never see each other again."

"And if I refuse?"

"Then you leave now. Empty-handed. Siobhan stays. And if you keep coming around, keep investigating, keep threatening my family... well. Venice Beach is full of people who disappear. One more won't matter."

The security guys waited. Ready.

I had no good options. No winning moves.

Just choices that all led to darkness.

"I need to think about it," I said.

"You have twenty-four hours. Then the offer expires. And so does your immunity."

They escorted me out.

I walked back to Echo Park in the late afternoon sun.

Thought about Emmett's offer.

Thought about becoming what I hunted to save someone who didn't want saving.

Thought about whether Declan's five hundred dollars was worth my soul.

Thought about David Emmett. And Siobhan Fury. And all the people caught in the machinery of other people's damage.

Got to my apartment.

Sat in the dark.

Made a decision.

Called Torres.

# Chapter 12: Morning After

**Torres met me at a different diner this time.**

San Pedro. Down by the docks. Far enough from Venice that we wouldn't be seen.

She was already in a booth when I arrived. Coffee in front of her. Looking tired.

I slid in across from her.

"You look like shit," she said.

"Didn't sleep."

"Undercover will do that." She studied me. "You sounded bad on the phone. What happened?"

I told her everything. The encampment. The nightwatch. The drug runs. The young women being sent out. The basement operation. Emmett's offer.

She listened without interrupting. Her cop face on. Taking it all in.

When I finished, she sat back.

"Jesus, Blair."

"Yeah."

"He's running a full operation. Drugs, prostitution, fraud. And using vulnerable people to do it."

"All disguised as ministry. As community service. Everyone thinks they're choosing it. Thinks it's their purpose."

"That's how these things work. Make exploitation feel like enlightenment."

The waitress came. Poured me coffee. Left without asking if we wanted food. Read the room correctly.

"The trade he offered," Torres said. "You're not actually considering it."

"I don't know what I'm considering."

"Blair. Listen to me. You can't trade yourself for her. That's insane. He'll never let either of you go. It's a trap."

"Probably."

"Definitely. He wants to destroy you. This is just another way to do it. Get you compromised. Get you dirty. Then either keep you or kill you."

She was right. I knew it.

"But what if he means it?" I said. "What if I could actually get her out?"

"You can't save her if she doesn't want saving. How many times do we have to go through this?"

"She only doesn't want saving because she's been manipulated. Brainwashed. If I could get her away from him, give her space to think—"

"Then what? She'd thank you? Go back to her father? Live happily ever after?" Torres shook her head. "That's not how it works. She'd resent you. Hate you. Go right back to Emmett the first chance she got."

I knew that too.

But knowing something and accepting it are different things.

"What about the evidence?" I asked. "What I saw. The drug runs. The prostitution. Can you use it?"

"Maybe. If we had witnesses willing to testify. If we had the actual drugs. If we had transactions we could trace. What you saw is enough for probable cause. But Emmett's smart. He's kept it just ambiguous enough that he can claim it's all voluntary. Adult choices. First Amendment protection."

"So we've got nothing."

"We've got something. Just not enough. Not yet."

"How much is enough?"

She thought about it. Drank her coffee. Looked out at the gray morning.

"We'd need someone from inside," she said finally. "Someone willing to flip. Someone who could testify about the coercion. The exploitation. The way Emmett controls people."

"None of them will flip. They all love him."

"Then we need to catch him in the act. Drugs in hand. Money changing hands. Something concrete and undeniable."

"And how do we do that?"

"You go back in. But not as his puppet. As our informant. You wear a wire. Document everything. Get him on tape admitting what he's doing."

"He'll know. He's already suspicious. The security guys would pat me down."

"Then we get creative. Plant surveillance in the house. Hidden cameras. Audio devices. Something he won't see coming."

"That requires warrants. Probable cause. All the things you said we don't have."

"It requires me risking my badge. Again."

She met my eyes.

"But I'm willing to do it. If you are."

"Why?"

"Because those women he's prostituting out? They deserve better. Because the people he's exploiting with his fake ministry deserve justice. Because your missing girl deserves a chance to wake up."

She said it like it was simple. Like risking her career and pension was just another Tuesday.

"I can't ask you to do that."

"You're not asking. I'm offering."

We sat there. Two people who'd worked together twelve years ago. Who'd survived each other's failures. Who kept showing up when the smart thing was to walk away.

"What's your plan?" I asked.

"I've got a contact in Vice. Owes me a favor. I can get surveillance equipment. Small cameras. Audio bugs. The kind that look like phone chargers or smoke detectors. We plant them in the house. See what we catch."

"And if we catch nothing?"

"Then at least we tried."

"And if we catch something but can't use it because it was illegally obtained?"

"Then we find another way. Anonymous tips. Parallel construction. The kind of gray area shit that makes Internal Affairs nervous but gets results."

This was the Torres I remembered. The one who believed the badge meant something beyond politics and bureaucracy. The one who'd risk everything to do the right thing.

Also the one who'd probably end up fired.

"You sure about this?" I asked.

"No. But I'm doing it anyway."

She pulled out her phone. Made a call. Spoke quietly. Hung up.

"My guy can meet us in two hours. Marina del Rey. He'll have the equipment."

"Just like that?"

"Just like that."

I drank my coffee. Thought about the next twenty-four hours. About Emmett's deadline. About the choice I'd have to make.

"I need to go back tonight," I said. "Tell him my decision."

"What are you going to tell him?"

"That I'll do it. Take the trade. Join his operation for a month."

"Blair—"

"But I'll be wired. I'll document everything. And when we have enough, we bring him down."

"That's suicide. If he finds the wire, if he suspects anything, you're dead."

"Yeah. But it's the only play that keeps Siobhan alive and gets us evidence."

She stared at me. "You're a fucking idiot."

"Probably."

"And you're going to get yourself killed."

"Maybe. But I made a promise."

"To who? Declan? He's paying you five hundred dollars. That's not worth your life."

"Not to Declan." I looked out the window. Watched the boats in the harbor. "To myself. That I wouldn't let another person disappear into a system that doesn't care. That I'd actually do something right for once."

Torres was quiet for a moment.

"The martyr complex doesn't suit you, Blair."

"Good thing I'm not trying to look good."

She smiled despite herself. Small smile. Sad.

"We do this, we do it right," she said. "Full planning. Backup. Exit strategy. I'm not losing another partner to bad decisions."

"I wasn't your partner when I fucked up. I was your training officer."

"Same difference. You taught me things. Some of them even useful."

"Like what?"

"Like the job matters more than the politics. Like sometimes you have to risk everything to do something right. Like good cops stay good by refusing to become what they fight."

Her words hit harder than she knew.

"I'm not sure I'm a good cop anymore, Torres. Not sure I ever was."

"Then prove it now. Go back in. Get the evidence. Save the girl. Don't die. In that order."

She stood up. Dropped money on the table.

"Marina del Rey. Two hours. Don't be late."

She left.

I sat there finishing my coffee.

Thought about Cormac McCarthy. About men choosing violence because peace wasn't available. About the machinery of evil that grinds people up and spits them out as statistics.

Emmett was that machinery. Built it himself out of grief and rage and the desire to hurt someone the way he'd been hurt.

I couldn't let him keep running it.

Even if stopping him meant becoming part of it.

Even if it killed me.

I paid my bill. Walked out into the San Pedro morning.

The harbor smelled like fish and diesel and the promise of elsewhere.

But I wasn't going elsewhere.

I was going back to Venice.

Back to Emmett.

Back into the dark.

Two hours later I met Torres in a Marina del Rey parking lot.

Her contact was there. Plainclothes cop, maybe thirty-five, looked like he'd seen things he wanted to forget. Name was Ramirez. Different Ramirez than the social worker.

"Torres says you need a wire," he said.

"Yeah."

"Going into a hostile environment?"

"Very."

He opened his trunk. Showed me the equipment. Small audio devices that looked like buttons. Cameras that looked like pen caps. A phone that wasn't just a phone.

"This stuff's cutting edge," he said. "Logs everything to cloud storage. Even if they find it and destroy it, we'll have the feed."

"How long does the battery last?"

"Seventy-two hours if you're careful. Less if you're streaming constantly."

"And if they find it?"

"Then it was nice knowing you."

Helpful.

He showed me how to activate it. How to hide it. How to make sure I was getting clean audio.

Torres watched. Silent. Her face unreadable.

"One more thing," Ramirez said. "This is off-book equipment. If you get caught with it, if this blows back, I was never here. You never met me. Understood?"

"Understood."

He handed me a small bag. Everything inside it.

"Good luck. Try not to die."

He got in his car. Drove away.

Torres and I stood in the parking lot.

"Last chance to back out," she said.

"I'm not backing out."

"I know. Just had to say it." She pulled out a card. Wrote a number on the back. "That's my personal cell. Not my work phone. You need anything, you call that. Day or night. I'll come."

"Thanks."

"And Blair? Don't be a hero. Get the evidence and get out. Don't try to save everyone. Just save her and yourself. That's enough."

"I'll try."

"No. You'll do it. Because if you die in there, I'm going to be pissed. And you don't want me pissed."

She hugged me. Quick. Hard. Then let go.

"Twenty-four hours," she said. "That's when you go back in. Use the time to prep. Rest. Get your head right."

"Will do."

She got in her car. Looked at me through the window.

"Don't make me regret this."

"Too late for that."

She drove away.

I stood there with a bag full of surveillance equipment and a plan that would probably get me killed.

Thought about calling Declan. Telling him I was close. Telling him his daughter would be free soon.

Didn't call.

Couldn't promise what I couldn't deliver.

Instead I went back to my apartment.

Showered. Shaved. Made coffee.

Practiced my story. My commitment speech. The lies I'd tell to get close enough to destroy Emmett's operation.

The lies that were also true.

I did want to save Siobhan. Did want to stop Emmett. Did want to do something right for once in my failed career and failing life.

The fact that it might kill me was just details.

Night came.

Tomorrow I'd accept Emmett's offer.

Tomorrow I'd become what I was fighting.

Tomorrow I'd step into the trap knowingly and hope I could spring it from inside.

I looked at the space where the Jameson bottle used to be.

Wished for it.

Didn't drink.

Five days sober now. Might be the last streak I ever got.

Might as well make it count.

# Chapter 13: The Dig

**I couldn't sleep.**

Three a.m. and I was at my laptop again. Digging through archives. Looking for something I'd missed. Some detail about David Emmett's death that would make sense of his brother's rage.

The original news story was brief. Man found hanged. Investigation pending. Family claims negligence.

But there had to be more.

I searched deeper. Found the coroner's report. Public record if you knew where to look.

David Michael Emmett. Age 31. Cause of death: asphyxiation by hanging. Manner: suicide.

But there were notes. Observations.

*Bruising on wrists consistent with restraints. Contusions on torso and face of unknown origin. Subject reported distress to guards multiple times in 72-hour period prior to death. Requests for medical evaluation denied due to staffing shortages.*

I read it twice.

Bruising. Contusions. Requests denied.

The official story was suicide. The reality looked like something else.

I kept digging.

Found the internal investigation report. Took some creative searching and a login I shouldn't have had. Old department credentials that someone forgot to deactivate.

The investigation cleared everyone. Guards followed procedure. No misconduct found. David Emmett was emotionally distressed, made multiple suicide threats, and ultimately followed through.

Case closed.

But the notes told a different story.

David had been placed in a cell with two other inmates. Both with violent histories. There had been an altercation on the second night. Guards broke it up. Moved David to isolation for his own protection.

That's where he hanged himself.

Except the timing didn't work.

He was found at 6 a.m. during morning rounds. But the last guard check was logged at 2 a.m. Four hours unobserved in isolation.

County jail was supposed to check isolation cells every thirty minutes.

Someone hadn't done their job.

Or had done it too well.

I found one more document. A complaint filed by Michael Emmett—before he became Prophet Emmett—alleging his brother was murdered by guards or inmates and the suicide ruling was a coverup.

The complaint was dismissed. Lack of evidence. Conflicting witness statements. The usual bureaucratic runaround.

Michael Emmett had tried to get justice for his brother through the system. The system had told him no.

So he'd built his own system. His own justice. His own way of making people pay.

I understood it now. The rage. The patience. The elaborate revenge.

Didn't excuse it. But I understood it.

My arrest had put David in that cell. My paperwork had set the chain of events in motion. Whether I pulled the bedsheet tight or not, I was part of the machinery that killed him.

Emmett was right about that.

I closed the laptop. Sat in the dark.

Thought about Don DeLillo. About how we're all part of systems we don't control. About how our smallest actions ripple out into consequences we never see.

I'd arrested thousands of people. Never thought about what happened to them after. Never considered that my job—just doing my job—might destroy lives.

That was the thing about being a cop. You processed people like paperwork. Moved them through the system. Told yourself it wasn't personal.

But it was always personal.

David Emmett had been someone's brother. Someone's son. Someone who mattered to someone.

And I hadn't even remembered his name.

The guilt sat heavy. Real. Deserved.

But guilt doesn't solve anything. Doesn't bring people back. Doesn't change the past.

Only thing guilt's good for is motivation.

And I was motivated now.

Not just to save Siobhan. Not just to take down Emmett's operation.

To make something right in a world where most things stay broken.

Dawn came gray and cold.

I showered. Made coffee. Ate something I didn't taste.

Prepared the surveillance equipment. The small camera hidden in a button. The audio device disguised as a zipper pull. The phone that logged everything to cloud storage.

Practiced activating them. Hiding them. Making them seem natural.

Torres called at eight.

"You ready?"

"As I'll ever be."

"Remember the protocol. Document everything. Don't try to be a hero. Get evidence and get out."

"I remember."

"And Blair? If it goes sideways, if you're in danger, you call me. Immediately. I don't care if you've got the evidence or not. You call."

"I will."

"Promise me."

"I promise."

She was quiet for a moment. "Good luck."

"Thanks."

She hung up.

I looked around my apartment. The studio that held my whole life. Books and coffee maker and Murphy bed and not much else.

Wondered if I'd see it again.

Wondered if that mattered.

Packed a small bag. Few clothes. Toiletries. The things Pete the homeless guy would have.

Hid the surveillance equipment in the lining. In the seams. In places they wouldn't look unless they stripped everything down to threads.

Left my apartment at ten a.m.

Drove to Venice for what might be the last time.

The encampment looked different in daylight. Less mysterious. More desperate. Just people living hard lives in public view.

Found Rachel distributing supplies.

"Pete! You came back."

"Yeah. Need to talk to Emmett."

"He's at the house. Said you might come by. Said to send you over when you did."

"Thanks."

I walked to the house. The surveillance equipment felt heavy in my bag. Heavy with possibility and danger.

Emmett was waiting outside. Like he knew exactly when I'd arrive.

"Pete. Right on time. You've made your decision?"

"Yeah. I'll do it. Take the trade. Work for the family for a month. Then you let Siobhan go."

He studied me. Looking for the lie. Looking for the angle.

"Why the change of heart?"

"Because you're right. I can't save her by force. Can't make her see what she doesn't want to see. But if I do this, if I prove I'm willing to sacrifice for her... maybe that means something. Maybe that's enough."

"Or maybe you're planning something. Some scheme to take me down while pretending to join us."

"I'm just trying to keep a promise to her father."

He smiled. "I almost believe you."

"Believe what you want. I'm here. I'm willing. What do I need to do?"

"First, you surrender everything. Wallet. Phone. Keys. Anything connecting you to your old life. You're part of the family now. The family provides everything you need."

I expected this. Handed over my regular phone. My wallet. My car keys.

Kept the burner phone hidden in my bag. The surveillance equipment concealed.

"Good. Second, you move into the house. You'll share a room with two other brothers. Communal living. No privacy. No secrets."

"Fine."

"Third, you do what you're told. When you're told. No questions. No hesitation. You're not an investigator anymore. You're not a cop. You're just another follower serving the family."

"Understood."

"And fourth..." He stepped closer. "You acknowledge what you did. To my brother. You admit your guilt. You carry that with you. Every day. Every task. You remember that you're here because of what you took from me."

His eyes were hard. Cold. This was the real price. Not the labor. Not the degradation. The guilt.

"I remember," I said. "I arrested your brother. He died in custody. I'm responsible."

"Say you're sorry."

"I'm sorry."

"Mean it."

I looked at him. Really looked at him. Saw the grief underneath the rage. Saw the brother who'd lost a brother. Saw the human inside the monster.

"I'm sorry," I said again. And meant it. "I'm sorry I didn't remember him. Sorry I treated him like paperwork. Sorry I was part of the system that killed him. I can't change it. Can't fix it. But I'm sorry."

Something shifted in his face. Not forgiveness. But acknowledgment.

"Good. That's a start." He extended his hand. "Welcome to the family, Pete. Let's see if you survive it."

I shook his hand.

Felt the trap close around me.

Felt the surveillance equipment pressing against my ribs.

Felt the weight of everything I was about to do.

Emmett led me inside. Showed me to my room. Small space with three sleeping bags on the floor. Introduced me to my roommates. Jason and Marcus. Both true believers. Both watching me with curiosity and caution.

"Get settled," Emmett said. "Rest. Tonight we've got work. Your first contribution to the family."

He left.

I sat on my sleeping bag. Unpacked my few things. Activated the audio device. The camera. Made sure they were recording.

Marcus and Jason watched.

"You're really doing this?" Jason asked. "Committing for real?"

"Yeah."

"Why?"

Good question.

"Because I need to prove something. To myself. That I can be part of something bigger."

They seemed to accept that. Nodded. Went back to their own activities.

I lay back. Stared at the ceiling.

Thought about the next month. About what I'd have to do. About how deep I'd have to go.

Thought about Siobhan. About whether this would actually save her.

Thought about Torres. About the backup that might not arrive in time.

Thought about David Emmett. About guilt and justice and the ways we try to balance scales that stay tilted.

My phone—the surveillance phone—buzzed quietly.

Text from Torres: *Signal's good. We're receiving. Stay safe.*

I texted back: *Will do.*

Deleted the exchange. Hid the phone.

Waited for night.

Waited for Emmett to tell me what my first contribution would be.

Waited to see how far I could go before I broke.

Or before he broke me.

Outside, Venice Beach kept selling itself.

Inside, I prepared to sell my soul.

For evidence.

For justice.

For a girl who didn't know she needed saving.

For a promise I'd made to myself more than anyone else.

The family would provide everything I needed, Emmett said.

Everything except a way out.

# Chapter 14: The Warning

**The first assignment came at nine p.m.**

Emmett found me in the communal area. I was helping clean up after dinner. Playing the role.

"Pete. Come with me."

I followed him to the basement. The command center.

His two security guys were already there. The ones I'd seen doing pickups. Names I'd learned: Cole and Brandon.

Both ex-military.

Both comfortable with violence.

"Tonight you make your first contribution," Emmett said. "Delivery run. Simple. You take a package from point A to point B. Bring back payment. Don't ask questions. Don't open the package. Just deliver."

"Where?"

"Cole will drive. You'll ride along. Learn the route. Next time you'll do it solo."

"What's in the package?"

"I said don't ask questions."

Drugs. Had to be. This was my first test. See if I'd follow orders. See if I'd cross the line.

The surveillance equipment was recording. This was exactly what Torres needed.

"Okay," I said. "I'll do it."

Emmett smiled. "Good. And Pete? Don't try anything stupid. Cole's armed. He's also under orders to make sure you come back. One way or another."

Cole patted his jacket. The bulge of a gun obvious.

"Understood."

"Excellent. You leave in ten minutes. There's a bag upstairs. Black duffel. Cole knows which one. Don't open it. Don't look inside it. Just deliver it and collect the payment."

He left us there. Cole and Brandon and me.

Cole grabbed the duffel from a closet. Heavy. Maybe ten pounds. Could be drugs. Could be money. Could be anything.

"Let's go," Cole said.

We walked to a van parked behind the house. White panel van. No markings. The kind of vehicle that's invisible by design.

Cole drove. I sat passenger seat. Brandon stayed behind.

We drove east. Out of Venice. Through Culver City. Into south LA.

Neighborhoods getting rougher as we went. Street lights broken. Businesses closed or boarded. The LA that tourists don't see.

Cole didn't talk. Just drove. Professional. Focused.

I kept the surveillance phone in my pocket. Audio recording everything. GPS tracking our route. Torres would know exactly where we went.

Thirty minutes later we pulled up to a house. Small. Run-down. Bars on the windows. Cars in the driveway that cost more than the house.

Drug dealer's house. Obvious.

"Stay in the van," Cole said. "I'll handle it."

"Emmett said I should learn the route. How do I learn if I stay in the van?"

He thought about it. "Fine. Come with me. But keep your mouth shut. Don't touch anything. Don't look at anyone directly. You're just the help. Understand?"

"Yeah."

We got out. Cole carried the duffel. I followed.

He knocked. Three quick raps. Two slow. Some kind of code.

The door opened. Man in his forties. Shaved head. Neck tattoos. Eyes that had seen everything and been impressed by nothing.

"Cole. On time for once."

"Always on time. You got the payment?"

"Let me see the product first."

Cole opened the duffel. Inside: plastic-wrapped packages. White powder visible through the clear wrapping. Had to be cocaine. Maybe five kilos.

I made sure to position myself where the button camera could see it. Documented everything.

The dealer checked a package. Nodded. Handed Cole an envelope.

"Twenty-five. Count it if you want."

"I trust you."

"No you don't. But Emmett does. So we're good."

They had history. This wasn't a first-time transaction. This was routine business.

Cole took the envelope. Handed over the duffel.

We walked back to the van.

"See?" Cole said. "Simple. You'll do this route twice a week. Tuesday and Friday. Pick up product from the house. Deliver here. Bring back payment. Keep your mouth shut about it and everyone's happy."

"Got it."

We drove back to Venice. Cole relaxed now that the delivery was done. Started talking.

"Been working for Emmett two years," he said. "Best job I ever had. Good money. Easy work. And he actually gives a shit about people."

"You believe in his mission? The family thing?"

"Don't care about the mission. Care about the paycheck. But yeah, he helps people. I've seen it. Takes homeless folks off the street. Gives them purpose. That's more than the city does."

"Even if the purpose is running drugs?"

"Everyone's running drugs. Least Emmett's honest about what he's doing. Doesn't pretend it's anything else. Just business."

"What about the young women? The ones who get sent out at night?"

His expression hardened. "That's voluntary. They choose it. Emmett doesn't force anyone."

"But he pressures them. Makes them think it's serving the family."

"So? Everyone pressures everyone. You think your old job didn't pressure you? Make you do shit you didn't want to do?" He glanced at me. "You were a cop, right? Before you fell apart?"

My cover was security work. But Cole knew different. Emmett had told him.

"Yeah. I was a cop."

"Then you know. System pressures people all the time. At least with Emmett, people get something back. Money. Community. Purpose. Better than what the state provides."

Hard to argue with that. The system had failed these people long before Emmett found them.

But that didn't make what he was doing right.

We got back to the house. Cole handed me the envelope.

"Give this to Emmett. Tell him delivery's done. No problems."

I took it. Went inside. Found Emmett in his office.

"How'd it go?"

"Fine. No problems." I handed him the envelope.

He opened it. Counted the cash. Twenty five thousand dollars. Twenties and hundreds. He didn't bother hiding it from me.

"Good. You did well. Next time you'll go solo. Prove you're trustworthy."

"What about the drugs? You're selling cocaine. That's—"

"That's business. The world wants drugs. I provide them. Same as any pharmaceutical company. Just more honest about it."

"People die from this shit."

"People die from lots of things. Poverty. Neglect. Hopelessness. I'm not the disease, Pete. I'm just a symptom." He put the money in his safe. "You got a problem with it?"

I thought about what to say. How much resistance to show. Too little and I seemed complicit. Too much and he'd suspect.

"I've got a problem with a lot of things. Doesn't mean I can fix them."

"Exactly. Can't fix the world. Can only make your corner of it better. That's what I'm doing."

He stood. Put his hand on my shoulder.

"You did good tonight. Proved you can follow orders. Proved you're serious about this. Keep it up and Siobhan walks free in twenty-eight days."

"That's the deal."

"That's the deal." He smiled. "Now get some rest. Tomorrow you've got outreach duty. Helping Rachel bring in new family members."

He dismissed me.

I went back to my room. Jason and Marcus were already asleep.

I lay on my sleeping bag. Pulled out the surveillance phone. Texted Torres.

*First delivery done. Cocaine run. South LA. Five kilos. 25k payment. All recorded.*

Her response came fast: *Good. Keep documenting. Don't take unnecessary risks.*

*Will do.*

I deleted the exchange.

Hid the phone.

Lay there thinking about what I'd just done.

I'd participated in a drug deal. Helped facilitate it. Made myself an accessory.

All for evidence. All to take down Emmett.

But the line between undercover work and criminal activity was getting blurry.

The law calls it "color of office." Says cops can break some laws to enforce others. But I wasn't a cop anymore. Was a PI doing illegal surveillance and facilitating drug trafficking.

If this went to court, if any of it became public, I'd be as guilty as Emmett.

Maybe more. Because I knew better.

But that was the price. The trade I'd made.

My integrity for evidence. My soul for justice. My freedom for Siobhan's.

Nicholas Pileggi wrote about wiseguys who thought they were doing good. Providing services the government wouldn't. Taking care of their communities. Justifying evil with small acts of kindness.

Emmett was a wiseguy with a messiah complex.

And I was becoming his accomplice.

Twenty-eight days.

If I could last that long.

If I could gather enough evidence.

If I could get out alive.

Sleep didn't come easy.

I lay there listening to Marcus snore.

Listening to Jason mumble in his dreams.

Listening to the house settle and creak.

Thinking about the drugs I'd just helped deliver. The lives they'd destroy. The system that made it all possible.

Thinking about Siobhan sleeping somewhere in this house. Believing she'd found purpose. Believing Emmett was saving her.

Not knowing she was part of the machinery. Part of the con.

Not knowing her salvation was someone else's trap.

Morning would come. More assignments. More tests. More lines to cross.

I'd cross them.

Document them.

Hope Torres could build a case before the whole thing collapsed.

Hope I could keep playing the role without becoming it.

Hope was a thin thing to hang your life on.

But it was all I had.

That and twenty-eight days.

If I survived them.

# Chapter 15: Lonnie's Advice

**I got out of the house the next morning.**

Told Emmett I needed air. Needed to walk. He watched me carefully but let me go. Probably had someone follow me. Didn't matter.

I walked to the Venice boardwalk. Found a pay phone. One of the last ones left. Relics of a time before everyone carried surveillance devices in their pockets.

Called Lonnie.

He answered on the third ring. "This is a number I don't know."

"It's Blair. Pay phone."

"Jesus. You in trouble?"

"Define trouble."

"Are you drinking?"

"No. Seven days sober."

"Then what?"

I looked around. Made sure no one was close enough to hear.

"I'm embedded in something. Undercover. Can't talk about details. But I'm doing things I shouldn't be doing. Becoming someone I don't want to be."

Silence on the line. Then: "You a cop again?"

"No. Private work. But it's... complicated."

"Complicated meaning illegal?"

"Complicated meaning I don't know anymore. The lines are blurry."

More silence. I could hear him thinking. Probably making coffee. Probably standing in his Malibu kitchen with the ocean view, trying to understand why his most problematic sponsee was calling from a pay phone talking about blurry lines.

"Why are you really calling?" he asked finally.

"Because I need someone to tell me I'm not crazy. That what I'm doing matters. That the ends justify the means."

"Can't do that."

"Why not?"

"Because the ends never justify the means. That's basic ethics. That's basic recovery. We don't do wrong things for right reasons. We just do right things and trust the outcome."

"That's easy to say when you're not in it."

"Nothing about recovery is easy. You know that." He paused. "What are you really asking me?"

Good question.

"I'm asking if it's okay to become a monster to fight monsters."

"And you know the answer already. You just don't like it."

"No."

"Then why call?"

"Because I need to hear it anyway. From someone who isn't compromised. Someone who still believes in things."

Lonnie sighed. "You want my advice? Real advice?"

"Yeah."

"Get out. Whatever you're doing, whoever you're helping, whatever case you're working—get out. Before you lose yourself completely. Before you become the thing you're fighting."

"I can't. I made a promise."

"To who?"

"To someone who needs help. To myself. To... I don't know. To the idea that I can still do something right."

"Blair. Listen to me. You're a good investigator. A decent man underneath all the damage. But you've got a martyr complex the size of LA. You think suffering for other people makes up for your past mistakes. It doesn't. It just creates new ones."

Same thing Torres said.

Everyone telling me the same truth.

"There's a girl," I said. "Twenty-three. Lost. Trapped in something she doesn't understand. Her father hired me to find her. I found her. But she doesn't want saving. She thinks she's found purpose."

"And you think you can save her anyway."

"I have to try."

"Why?"

Another good question.

"Because no one tried to save me. When I was drinking myself to death. When I was destroying my career. My relationships. My life. No one grabbed me and made me see what I was doing. I had to hit bottom on my own. And I almost didn't survive it."

"So you're trying to save her from hitting bottom."

"Yeah."

"That's not how it works. You know that. People have to want to be saved. Have to choose recovery themselves. You can't force it."

"I know. But what if the bottom kills her? What if she doesn't get a chance to choose?"

Lonnie was quiet for a long time.

"Then you do what you can," he said finally. "But you don't sacrifice yourself in the process. Don't become what you're fighting. Don't cross lines you can't uncross. Because if you destroy yourself saving her, you've saved no one."

"What if I've already crossed those lines?"

"Then you stop. Now. Before you go further."

"It's not that simple."

"It's exactly that simple. You just don't want it to be."

He was right. As usual.

"I've got twenty-seven days left," I said. "Then it's done. Then she walks free."

"And what about you? Do you walk free?"

"Don't know yet."

"That's what I'm worried about." His voice softened. "You still going to meetings?"

"Can't. I'm embedded. Living in a house with true believers. No privacy. No time alone except right now."

"Then you're white-knuckling it. Dry but not sober. That's dangerous, Blair."

"Everything about this is dangerous."

"All the more reason to have a foundation. To have a program. To have something keeping you grounded."

I looked out at the ocean. The Pacific stretching to the horizon. Indifferent to all the small human struggles happening on its shore.

"I'm doing the best I can," I said.

"I know. But your best sometimes kills you. That's what I'm trying to prevent."

A man walked past. Glanced at me. Kept walking. Could've been one of Emmett's people. Could've been nobody.

"I have to go," I said.

"Blair. One more thing."

"Yeah?"

"You remember what we say in meetings? 'We're only as sick as our secrets'? Whatever you're hiding, whatever you're doing—it's eating you. I can hear it in your voice. Sobriety won't survive this. You won't survive this. Not if you keep it all locked up."

"I can't talk about it. Not yet. Not until it's done."

"Then call me when it is done. Call me before you drink. Call me before you do something stupid. Just call."

"I will."

"Promise me."

"I promise."

"Good. Now get out of there. Before it's too late."

"Twenty-seven days, Lonnie."

"That's a long time to stay undercover. A long time to pretend to be someone you're not. Just remember: you pretend long enough, you become it. That's not wisdom. That's warning."

He hung up.

I stood there holding the phone. Listening to the dial tone.

Put it back on the hook.

Walked back toward the house.

Thought about what Lonnie said.

About becoming what you pretend to be.

About crossing lines you can't uncross.

Thought about last night. The cocaine delivery. The twenty-five thousand dollars. My participation in it all.

Thought about the surveillance equipment recording everything. Torres building a case. The evidence mounting.

Thought about whether any of it mattered if I destroyed myself getting it.

Graham Greene wrote about whiskey priests and damaged saints. People trying to do good while being complicit in evil. The moral weight of compromise.

I understood those characters now. Understood the impossible choices. The way you try to serve something bigger while serving yourself. The way intentions and actions pull in opposite directions.

I was a whiskey priest without the whiskey. A damaged saint without the sanctity.

Just a man trying to save someone who didn't want saving while losing himself in the process.

Classic noir shit.

I got back to the house. Rachel was waiting.

"Pete! Perfect timing. We're doing outreach today. Bringing supplies to the encampments. Meeting new people who might need the family. Want to come?"

"Sure."

"Great! It's my favorite part. Seeing people's faces when they realize they're not alone. That someone cares."

She was genuine. Really believed in what they were doing. Really thought Emmett was helping people.

That made it harder.

Because she wasn't wrong. Not completely. Emmett did help people. Did give them community and purpose and hope.

He just extracted a price for it. Used them. Exploited their vulnerability.

But to Rachel, to most of the family, that part was invisible. Hidden behind the good works and the warm rhetoric and the feeling of belonging.

We loaded a van with supplies. Food. Water. Blankets. The basics.

Drove to encampments in different parts of LA. Places where homeless populations concentrated. Under freeway overpasses. In parking lots. Along riverbeds.

Rachel worked each site like a professional. Distributed supplies. Talked to people. Listened to their stories. Offered them connection to the family.

Some were interested. Some were suspicious. Some just wanted the food and water.

I helped. Carried boxes. Made conversation. Played the role of reformed addict finding purpose in service.

And the surveillance equipment documented everything.

The recruitment techniques. The way Rachel identified vulnerable people. The way she made initial contact. The way she slowly introduced the idea of Emmett and the family.

It was textbook cult recruitment.

Except it was also genuine community outreach.

Both things true at once.

That was the genius of it. Hide the exploitation inside actual charity. Make the con indistinguishable from the kindness.

After six hours we returned to the house. Rachel was glowing. Happy. Fulfilled.

"We helped so many people today," she said. "Did you feel it? The connection? The purpose?"

"Yeah," I said. "I felt it."

And I did. That was the terrible part.

Part of me wanted what they had. The certainty. The belonging. The simplicity of knowing your role and playing it without question.

Part of me envied their delusion.

That part scared me more than anything else.

Emmett found me later. Evening. I was helping prepare dinner.

"How was outreach with Rachel?"

"Good. She's dedicated."

"She is. One of my best recruiters. She genuinely cares. That's why people trust her." He smiled. "You did well today. Contributing without complaining. That's what family means."

"Just doing what needs doing."

"Exactly. Keep that attitude and we'll be fine. You, me, Siobhan. Everyone gets what they want."

He walked away.

I finished cutting vegetables. Helped serve dinner. Ate with the family.

Watched Siobhan laugh with her friends. Watched Rachel glow with purpose. Watched Marcus and Jason and all the others live their lives inside Emmett's carefully constructed reality.

Watched and documented and wondered how much longer I could keep this up.

Twenty-seven days seemed like forever.

Seemed like not long enough.

That night I texted Torres: *Outreach documented. Recruitment tactics on camera. Need to talk soon.*

Her response: *Meet tomorrow. 6am. Same diner in San Pedro. Can you get away?*

*Will try.*

I deleted the exchange.

Lay on my sleeping bag.

Thought about Lonnie's warning. About becoming what you pretend to be.

Thought about how good it felt today. Helping people. Being part of something.

Thought about how easy it would be to stop pretending.

To just become Pete. Just another lost soul who found family.

To forget about Peter Blair. Forget about the investigation. Forget about the surveillance equipment hidden in my bag.

To surrender.

That's what scared me most.

Not Emmett. Not the danger. Not the criminal activity.

The fact that part of me wanted to stay.

Wanted to believe.

Wanted to belong.

I closed my eyes.

Promised myself I'd make it to that meeting.

Promised myself I'd remember who I was.

Promised myself I wouldn't become what I was pretending to be.

Twenty-seven days.

Just had to last twenty-seven more days.

Without losing myself completely.

Without forgetting why I came.

Without surrendering to the same lie that trapped Siobhan.

Simple.

Except nothing about this was simple anymore.

# Chapter 16: The Approach

**I told Emmett I needed to go to an AA meeting.**

Morning. After breakfast. He was in his office counting money from last night's deliveries.

"A meeting," he repeated. Not a question. A test.

"Yeah. Been over a week since my last one. Need to stay grounded."

"The family should be your grounding now."

"The family's great. But I'm an addict. I need the program. You want me to stay sober, I need meetings."

He studied me. Weighing whether this was legitimate or an escape attempt.

"Where's the meeting?"

"There's one in Santa Monica. Six-thirty a.m. I can be back by eight."

"Cole will drive you."

"I'd rather walk. Part of the meditation. The routine."

"Cole drives you. Waits outside. Brings you back. That's the deal."

Not ideal. But workable.

"Okay."

Twenty minutes later Cole and I were in the van. Driving north toward Santa Monica.

He dropped me at a church. Real AA meeting location. I'd done my research.

"One hour," he said. "I'll be here."

"Thanks."

I went inside. The meeting was real. Early birds and insomniacs and people clinging to sobriety like a life raft.

I sat in back. Listened to shares. Nodded at the familiar rhythms. The same stories told different ways. The same struggles. The same hope.

But I wasn't really there.

Fifteen minutes in, I got up.

Went to the bathroom.

Climbed out the window.

Old trick. Simple. Effective.

Ran three blocks. Found a bus stop. Caught the bus to San Pedro.

Made it to the diner by six-fifteen.

Torres was waiting. Same booth. Same tired expression.

I slid in across from her.

"You look worse," she said.

"Feel worse."

"How bad is it?"

"Bad. I'm facilitating drug deals. Living with criminals. Pretending to be someone I'm not. And the worst part? Part of me likes it."

"Likes what?"

"The belonging. The purpose. The simplicity of just following orders and believing in something."

She reached across the table. Put her hand on mine. Rare
gesture. Meant she was worried.

"You're in too deep. Pull out. We've got enough for a case."

"Do we?"

"We've got you on camera documenting drug trafficking. We've got recordings of Emmett discussing the operation. We've got evidence of recruitment and exploitation. It's
enough to start building something."

"But not enough to convict. Not enough to shut him down
permanently."

"Maybe not. But enough to get warrants. Enough to bring
in the task force. Enough to save the people trapped in there."

I thought about Siobhan. About twenty-seven days. About
the deal I'd made.

"I need to finish this. Need to see it through."

"Why? Because you made some promise to yourself? Because you think suffering proves something?"

"Because if I pull out now, she stays trapped. If I finish the
month, Emmett lets her go. That was the deal."

"And you believe him? You think he'll actually honor that?"

"I don't know. But I have to try."

Torres pulled her hand back. Leaned back in the booth.

"You're going to get killed. You know that, right? Either
Emmett will figure out you're wired and put you in the ground.
Or you'll get so lost in the role you'll forget which side you're
on. Either way, you don't come out of this intact."

"I know."

"And you're doing it anyway."

"Yeah."

She shook her head. "You're an idiot."

"So I've been told."

The waitress came. Poured coffee. We ordered breakfast neither of us would finish.

"Tell me what else you've documented," Torres said.

I walked her through it.

The deliveries. The recruitment. The house operations. The money. The systematic exploitation wrapped in community service.

She took notes. Asked questions. Built her case in real time.

"This is good," she said. "Better than I expected. If you can keep this up for another few weeks, we'll have everything we need."

"And then what?"

"Then we move. Task force raid. Arrest Emmett and his security guys. Rescue the victims. Shut it down."

"What about the people who believe in it? Rachel and Marcus and all the others who think they've found salvation?"

"They'll be angry. Confused. Lost. But they'll be free. Sometimes freedom looks like devastation at first."

She was right. But that didn't make it easier.

"I need to get back," I said. "Cole's waiting at the meeting. When I don't show up, he'll start looking."

"How'd you slip him?"

"Bathroom window. Classic."

"He's going to be pissed."

"Yeah. But I'll tell him I had a panic attack. Needed to walk. Couldn't handle being inside. He'll buy it. Addicts are unpredictable."

Torres finished her coffee. "Check in every day. Text me. Let me know you're alive. If I don't hear from you for twenty-four hours, I'm coming in."

"Deal."

We stood. She hugged me. Quick and hard.

"Don't die in there, Blair."

"I'll try not to."

"And don't forget who you are. That's what Lonnie said, right? Don't become what you're pretending to be."

"Right."

I left. Caught the bus back to Santa Monica. Got there fifteen minutes after the meeting ended.

Cole was waiting. Leaning against the van. Smoking. Looking annoyed.

"Where the fuck were you?"

"Panic attack. Couldn't stay inside. Walked around the block. I'm sorry."

He studied me. Looking for the lie.

"You disappeared on me again, we're going to have problems. Emmett doesn't like people he can't track."

"Understood. Won't happen again."

We drove back to Venice in silence.

When we got to the house, Emmett was waiting.

"How was the meeting?"

"Good. Needed. Thanks for letting me go."

"Cole says you disappeared."

"Panic attack. Too many people. Needed air. Sorry."

Emmett looked at Cole. Cole shrugged. Seemed plausible to him.

"Next time, tell Cole first. We don't like mysteries in this family."

"Will do."

He let it go. But I could feel his suspicion. Feel the trust eroding.

I went to my room. Jason and Marcus were out. I had a few minutes alone.

Checked the surveillance equipment. Still recording. Still uploading to Torres's server.

Deleted my text history. Hid the phone.

Lay back on my sleeping bag.

Thought about the meeting with Torres. About the evidence we'd gathered. About the endgame coming into focus.

Twenty-seven days.

If I could make it.

That afternoon I was helping in the kitchen when Siobhan came in.

We'd been in the same house for days but barely interacted. She was part of the inner circle. I was new recruit. Different orbits.

But now it was just us. Alone in the kitchen.

She was making tea. I was washing dishes.

"You're Pete, right?" she said.

"Yeah. Siobhan?"

"How'd you know my name?"

"Rachel mentioned you. Said you were one of the committed ones."

She smiled. "I try to be. This place saved my life."

"How so?"

She poured hot water over a tea bag. Watched it steep.

"My mom died two years ago. Cancer. After that I was... lost. Didn't know who I was. Didn't know why anything mattered. I was drowning and didn't even know it."

"I'm sorry."

"Thanks. But it's okay now. I found the family. Found Emmett. Found purpose. The grief's still there, but it's bearable now. Because I'm part of something bigger."

I wanted to grab her. Shake her. Tell her it was all a lie. Tell her Emmett was using her. Tell her father was desperate to find her.

Instead I said, "That's good. Having purpose helps."

"What about you? What brought you here?"

"Similar story. Lost everything. Job. Apartment. Sense of self. Was living rough until Rachel found me."

"She's good at that. Finding people who need us."

"She is."

We stood there. Two people making small talk. Except I knew things she didn't. Knew her father. Knew the truth about Emmett. Knew this whole thing was temporary for me and permanent for her.

"Can I ask you something?" she said.

"Sure."

"Do you ever miss your old life? Before this?"

Loaded question. She was testing me. Or testing herself.

"Sometimes. But the old life was killing me. This is better. Harder in some ways. But better."

"That's how I feel. My old life looked fine from outside. But inside I was dying. This is real. This is alive."

She believed every word.

That was the tragedy of it.

"Your family must worry about you," I said carefully. "People from your old life."

Her expression hardened slightly. "I had a father. We weren't close. He was absent most of my life. Drunk. Selfish. Now he pretends to care. But it's too late."

"People change. Maybe he's different now."

"Maybe. But I've changed too. I'm not the person he thinks I am. I'm not his daughter anymore. I'm part of this family. That's who I am now."

She finished her tea. Rinsed the cup. Left the kitchen.

I stood there. Alone. Thinking about what she'd said.

She'd rewritten her history. Made Declan the villain. Made her abandonment of him righteous instead of tragic.

Classic cult psychology. Sever old attachments. Reinforce new identity. Make leaving impossible by burning all bridges.

Emmett had done his work well.

That night I texted Torres: *Talked to Siobhan. She's fully committed. Doesn't want contact with her father. This is harder than I thought.*

Her response: *Stay focused. You're not there to convince her. You're there to build evidence. Let the evidence speak for itself.*

*Roger that.*

But it didn't feel that simple.

Because Siobhan wasn't just evidence. She was a person. A daughter. Someone who'd lost her mother and found false comfort in a con man's arms.

And I was running out of time to save her.

Twenty-six days left.

The house settled into evening routines. Dinner. Cleaning. Prayer circle led by Emmett.

I participated. Played the role. Documented everything.

Felt myself slipping further into the character of Pete.

Felt Peter Blair getting smaller. More distant.

Leonard Cohen wrote about everybody knowing the dice are loaded. About the ship sinking. About fighting on even when you know you're losing.

I was fighting.

But I wasn't sure for what anymore.

For Siobhan? For Declan? For myself?

For the idea that I could still do something right in a world where most things stayed broken?

All of it. None of it.

Just fighting because that's what you do.

Because stopping means surrendering.

And I wasn't ready to surrender yet.

Not to Emmett. Not to the role. Not to the darkness.

Twenty-six days.

I could make it.

Had to make it.

No other choice left.

# Chapter 17: The Bottle

**It happened on day twelve.**

I'd been doing well. Following orders. Making deliveries. Documenting everything. Playing the role of committed follower. Staying sober despite the pressure.

Eight days sober when I came in. Twenty days now. A decent streak.

Then it all fell apart.

The delivery run went wrong.

Cole and I drove to the usual house. Same dealer. Same routine. Five kilos of cocaine for twenty-five thousand cash.

Except this time the cops were waiting.

We pulled up. Cole got out with the duffel. I stayed in the van like always.

Three steps to the door. Then: "Police! Down on the ground!"

Five cops. Full tactical gear. Guns drawn.

Cole dropped the duffel. Hands up. Getting on the ground.

I froze. Hands on the wheel. Every instinct screaming *RUN*.

But I couldn't. Pete wouldn't run. Pete would be scared and confused and compliant.

So I stayed.

A cop yanked open my door. Pulled me out. Face-first against the van.

"Don't move! Hands behind your back!"

Handcuffs. Cold metal. The familiar bite.

They searched me. Found my burner phone. The surveillance phone.

My stomach dropped.

Found it and bagged it. Evidence.

"What's this?" the cop asked.

"My phone."

"Locked. What's the code?"

"I don't have to tell you that."

He smiled. "No. You don't. We'll get a warrant. See what's on here."

They searched the van. Found the duffel. Five kilos. Street value quarter million.

Cole stayed quiet. Didn't say anything. Didn't look at me.

Professional.

They loaded us into separate cars. Took us downtown.

I sat in the back of the police cruiser thinking about Torres. About whether this was her move. Whether she'd coordinated the bust.

Whether I was going to jail or being extracted.

Couldn't tell.

At the station they separated us. Put me in an interview room.

I waited.

An hour passed. Two.

Finally the door opened.

Torres walked in.

Relief hit me like a wave.

"You okay?" she asked.

"What the fuck just happened?"

"Narcotics ran their own operation. Didn't coordinate with me. Didn't know you were undercover. They saw the pattern, set up surveillance, made the bust."

"Jesus Christ."

"I'm getting you out. Talked to the lieutenant. Explained you're my CI. Working a bigger case. They're not happy, but they'll release you."

"What about Cole?"

"He's getting booked. Possession with intent. He'll make bail by morning. Emmett will take care of it."

"And the phone? The surveillance evidence?"

"We got it back. I told them it's part of our investigation. Couldn't let them unlock it. Too much sensitive information."

She sat down across from me. Looked tired.

"This is a problem, Blair. You being arrested. Cole seeing you get released. Emmett's going to know something's wrong."

"What do I tell him?"

"Tell him the truth. Sort of. Tell him you got arrested. Tell him the cops questioned you. Tell him you didn't say anything. Played it smart. Got released because they didn't have enough to hold you."

"He won't buy it."

"He might. Cops release people all the time. Paperwork errors. Overcrowding. Technicalities. It happens."

"Or he'll think I flipped. Think I'm cooperating. Think I'm a rat."

"Yeah. That's the risk."

We sat there. The interview room familiar and foreign at the same time. I'd been on both sides of this table. Cop and suspect. Hunter and prey.

Now I was something else. Something in between.

"I need to pull you out," Torres said. "This is blown. Too dangerous to continue."

"No. I can salvage this. Play it right. Make Emmett believe me."

"And if he doesn't? If he decides you're a liability?"

"Then I deal with it."

"By getting killed?"

"By finishing what I started."

She stared at me. "You're going to get yourself killed for a girl who doesn't want saving."

"Maybe. But I made a promise."

"Fuck your promise. I'd rather have you alive and guilty than dead and righteous."

"You don't get a vote."

"The hell I don't. I'm the one who got you the equipment. I'm the one who's been building the case. I'm the one who'll have to explain to your sponsor why you died in a cult compound in Venice Beach."

Her voice cracked on the last part. Barely. But I heard it.

"I'm not going to die."

"You don't know that."

"No. But I'm going back anyway."

She stood up. Paced the small room.

"You've got twenty-four hours," she said finally. "Twenty-four hours to convince Emmett you're solid. If you can't, if he suspects anything, you call me. Immediately. And I pull you out. By force if necessary."

"Deal."

"I mean it, Blair. I'm not losing another partner to stubbornness."

"I was never your partner. I was your training officer."

"Same fucking thing." She opened the door. "You're free to go. Get out of here before I change my mind and book you myself."

I stood. Walked toward the door. Stopped.

"Torres. Thank you."

"Don't thank me. Just don't die."

I left the station. Evening now. The city dark and indifferent.

Called a cab. Gave the driver the Venice address.

Sat in the back thinking about what I'd tell Emmett. How I'd play it. Whether it would work.

Whether I'd survive the night.

The cab dropped me three blocks from the house. I walked the rest.

Every step felt heavier.

Cole's van was already there. He'd made bail fast. Emmett's money working efficiently.

I walked in the front door.

Everyone stopped. Looked at me.

Emmett emerged from the office. Cole beside him.

"Pete. We need to talk."

I followed them to the basement. The command center. Cole closed the door behind us.

"Cole says you got released," Emmett said. "Two hours after arrest. No bail. No charges. Just walked out."

"Yeah."

"Explain that."

"Paperwork error. They thought I was someone else. Ran my prints. Saw I had no warrants. Let me go."

"While keeping Cole."

"Cole had the drugs. I was just in the van. They couldn't charge me with anything."

Emmett studied me. Looking for tells. Looking for lies.

"And they didn't ask you questions? Didn't try to flip you?"

"They asked. I didn't answer. Lawyer-ed up. Stayed quiet."

"What about your phone? The one they took?"

My heart rate spiked. Kept my face neutral.

"What about it?"

"Did they look through it?"

"They wanted the code. I didn't give it. Said they'd need a warrant."

"And if they get a warrant? If they unlock it? What will they find?"

"Nothing. It's a burner. No contacts. No history. Just a phone."

Cole spoke for the first time. "He's lying. Has to be. Nobody gets released that fast unless they cooperate."

"I didn't cooperate."

"Then how'd you get out?"

"I told you. Paperwork error. Overcrowding. They process hundreds of people a day. Shit gets confused."

Emmett held up his hand. Silence.

"Here's what I think," he said. "Either you're telling the truth and you got lucky. Or you're lying and you flipped. Either way, I have a problem."

"What problem?"

"Trust. You've been here less than two weeks. Now you're getting arrested and mysteriously released. That makes me nervous. And when I'm nervous, I make changes."

"What kind of changes?"

"The kind where you prove yourself. Right now. Tonight."

He opened a drawer. Pulled out a gun. Placed it on the desk between us.

"Tomorrow night you're going on a delivery. Different route. Different dealer. Higher stakes. You'll carry product worth half a million. Bring back the cash. And you'll go alone. No Cole. No backup. Just you."

"Why alone?"

"Because if you're solid, you'll do it. If you're working with cops, you'll try to set up another bust. And we'll know."

The trap was elegant. If I did it, I was deeper in. If I didn't, I was exposed. If I tried to coordinate with Torres, Emmett would have people watching. Waiting to see if cops showed up.

No winning moves.

"Okay," I said. "I'll do it."

"Good. And Pete? If you fuck this up, if you betray this family, I won't just kill you. I'll make sure Siobhan knows exactly who you are. What you did to my brother. How you infiltrated us to destroy everything we built. She'll hate you. More than she hates her father. More than she hates her old life. You'll die knowing you destroyed any chance she had at peace."

He picked up the gun. Handed it to me.

"You'll need this. The dealers you're meeting aren't like the others. They're dangerous. Unstable. You might have to defend yourself."

I took the gun. Felt the weight of it.

"What time tomorrow?"

"Eleven p.m. Cole will give you the address. You go alone. Do the deal. Come back alive with the money. Prove you're family."

He dismissed me.

I went upstairs. To my room. Jason and Marcus were there. Talking quietly. Stopped when I came in.

Word had spread. The new guy got arrested. Got released suspiciously fast. Now he's suspect.

I lay on my sleeping bag. Stared at the ceiling.

Thought about tomorrow night. About the half-million-dollar delivery. About the gun in my bag.

About how far I'd fallen into this.

Thought about calling Torres. Telling her to pull me out.

Couldn't. Not yet.

Had to do this delivery. Had to prove myself. Had to keep the cover intact long enough to finish what I started.

Twenty-five days left.

Might as well be twenty-five years.

I pulled out the surveillance phone. Hidden. Checked for messages.

Torres: *Are you okay? Status update needed.*

I couldn't text back. Not here. Not with Jason and Marcus watching.

Would have to wait until I could slip away.

Lay there until the house went quiet.

Until everyone slept.

Then I got up. Grabbed my jacket. Walked outside.

Found a pay phone two blocks away.

Called Torres.

"Blair. Jesus. You okay?"

"For now. But Emmett's testing me. Big delivery tomorrow night. Half a million in product. Alone. If I don't do it, I'm exposed. If I do it, I'm accessory to major trafficking."

"Then don't do it. Pull out. We've got enough evidence."

"Not enough to convict. Not enough to shut him down permanently."

"Who cares? You'll be alive."

"The delivery's the proof. Him trusting me with that much product. That's conspiracy. That's the top charge. That's what puts him away for twenty years."

"Or it's the thing that gets you killed."

"Maybe."

She was quiet. Then: "I can't protect you if you do this. Can't coordinate a bust. Can't have cops waiting. Emmett will have people watching. You'll be completely on your own."

"I know."

"This is insane."

"Yeah."

"And you're doing it anyway."

"Yeah."

More silence. Then: "If you die doing this, I'm going to kill you."

"Fair."

"Call me after. Immediately after. Let me know you survived."

"Will do."

"And Blair? Be careful. Please."

"I'll try."

I hung up. Started walking back.

Passed a liquor store. Still open. Late night special.

Stopped.

Looked in the window. Rows of bottles. Amber and clear. Promises in glass.

I hadn't had a drink in twenty days.

Twenty days of white-knuckling it. Of pretending to be someone else. Of crossing lines and documenting crimes and losing myself in the role.

Twenty days of being strong.

I was tired of being strong.

Walked into the store. Bought a pint of Jameson. Paid cash. Walked out.

Stood on the street corner. Looked at the bottle.

Thought about Lonnie. About Torres. About promises I'd made.

Thought about Siobhan. About Declan. About doing something right for once.

Thought about all the reasons not to drink.

Unscrewed the cap.

Drank.

The burn was familiar. Welcome. Like coming home to a house you hate but can't leave.

Drank more.

Walked back to the house. Finished the bottle on the way. Threw it in a dumpster.

Arrived drunk. First time in twenty days.

Felt like failure. Felt like relief.

Felt like nothing at all.

Went to my room. Jason and Marcus asleep.

Lay down. The room spinning slightly.

Tomorrow I'd do a half-million-dollar drug delivery.

Tomorrow I'd risk my life for evidence.

Tomorrow I'd prove myself to a man who wanted to destroy me.

But tonight I was drunk.

Tonight I'd failed.

Again.

John Fante wrote about asking the dust for help. About falling down and getting back up. About surviving Los Angeles when Los Angeles wanted you dead.

I was falling down.

Hoping I'd get back up.

Knowing I might not.

Twenty days sober. Gone.

Just like everything else.

Sleep came ugly and dark.

Tomorrow would be worse.

# Chapter 18: Torres Decides

**I woke up with a hangover and a plan to die.**

Not intentionally. But the half-million-dollar delivery tonight had those odds.

The room was empty. Jason and Marcus already up. Probably avoiding me. Word had spread about the arrest. About the suspicion. About Emmett's test.

I was radioactive now.

Good.

I sat up. Head pounding. Mouth dry. The familiar consequences of familiar mistakes.

Twenty days sober. Gone in one night.

But I didn't have time for self-pity. Had work to do.

Found my surveillance phone. Hidden in the lining of my bag. Checked messages.

Torres: *Call me. Now.*

I went outside. Found a spot behind the house where no one could see me. Called.

She answered immediately.

"You sound like shit."

"Feel like shit."

"Did you drink?"

Silence. She knew the answer.

"Goddammit, Blair."

"I know."

"You know? That's all you've got? After everything—after Lonnie, after the work, after twenty days—you just threw it away?"

"I didn't throw it away. I lost it. There's a difference."

"Not from where I'm sitting." Her voice was hard. Angry. "You're compromised. Drunk. Heading into a half-million-dollar drug deal tonight. This is suicide."

"Maybe."

"Maybe? That's your answer?"

"What do you want me to say, Torres? That I'm sorry? That I'll do better? I'm out of apologies. I'm out of promises. I'm just trying to survive until tonight."

She was quiet. Then: "Where are you right now? Physically."

"Behind the house. Alone."

"Can you get away? Meet me?"

"Why?"

"Because we need to talk face-to-face. Because I need to see if you're functional enough to do this. Because I'm not letting you walk into that delivery drunk and stupid."

"I'm not drunk anymore. Just hungover."

"Same thing. Can you get away or not?"

I looked around. The house was waking up. People moving around. Emmett would be watching me today. Making sure I didn't run.

"I can try. Where?"

"Same diner. San Pedro. One hour."

"Torres, I can't just—"

"One hour. Figure it out."

She hung up.

I stood there. Thinking about how to slip away. About what lie would work.

Went back inside. Found Emmett in the kitchen.

"Morning," he said. Watching me.

"Morning."

"Big night tonight. You ready?"

"Ready as I'll be."

"Good. Stay close today. Rest. Prepare. Cole will brief you this afternoon on the route."

"Actually, I need to go out. Clear my head. Walk the beach. Get centered."

His eyes narrowed. "Not sure that's a good idea. Given yesterday's events."

"I'm not running. Where would I go? You've got my real phone. My wallet. My keys. I'm trapped here same as everyone else."

"Trapped is a strong word."

"Is it?"

He studied me. "One hour. You've got one hour to walk. Then you come back. And you stay until tonight. Clear?"

"Clear."

"Cole will follow you. At a distance. Just to make sure you're walking like you said. Not meeting anyone. Not making calls."

Of course.

"Fine."

I left. Started walking toward the beach. Felt Cole's presence behind me. Fifty yards back. Watching.

Kept walking. Let him think I was just walking.

Then I ducked into a coffee shop. Went straight through to the back. Out the rear exit. Into an alley.

Ran.

Three blocks. Four. Lost Cole in the Venice morning crowd.

Caught a bus. Made it to San Pedro in forty minutes.

Torres was waiting. Same booth. Same diner. Different level of pissed.

I slid in across from her.

She looked at me. Really looked. Taking inventory.

"You look terrible."

"Thanks."

"Hungover?"

"Yeah."

"How much did you drink?"

"A pint. Give or take."

"Jesus, Blair."

The waitress came. Coffee. Water. I drank both like I'd crossed a desert.

Torres waited until I'd emptied the water glass.

"I'm pulling you out," she said.

"No."

"That wasn't a question. I'm pulling you out. Tonight. Before the delivery. This is done."

"You can't. I need to do this. Need to prove myself to Emmett. Need to—"

"Need to get yourself killed? Mission accomplished. You're drunk, compromised, and walking into a setup that's designed to either expose you or eliminate you. I'm not letting it happen."

"It's not your call."

"The hell it's not. I'm the one who got you the equipment. I'm the one who's been protecting you from my department. I'm the one who has to live with it if you die in there."

"I'm not going to die."

"You don't know that. You're impaired. Emotionally. Physically. Mentally. You're in no condition to do a high-stakes drug deal with dangerous people while pretending to be someone you're not."

She was right. About all of it.

But that didn't change anything.

"I have to finish this," I said. "Have to see it through. For Siobhan. For Declan. For myself."

"For yourself? This isn't about you. This is about some misguided need to prove you're not a fuckup. But guess what? You are a fuckup. We all are. That doesn't mean you have to die proving otherwise."

Her words hit hard. True and harsh.

"I made a deal with Emmett," I said quietly. "Do this for a month. Prove myself. Then Siobhan goes free. I'm halfway there. Can't quit now."

"You really think he'll honor that deal? You really think after all this, he'll just let her walk?"

"I don't know. But I have to try."

Torres leaned back. Rubbed her face. Tired. Frustrated. Worried.

"You're the most stubborn son of a bitch I've ever met."

"So I've been told."

"And you're not going to back down on this."

"No."

She sat there.

Thinking. Processing. Making decisions

I couldn't see.

"Okay," she said finally. "Here's what's going to happen. You do the delivery. But you're not going in alone."

"Emmett said—"

"I don't care what Emmett said. You're not going in alone. I'll have plainclothes nearby. Not close enough to spook anyone. But close enough to move if things go bad."

"He'll have people watching. Looking for exactly that."

"Then we'll be careful. Invisible. You won't even know we're there."

"Torres, if he sees cops, if he suspects anything, it's over. He'll kill me. He'll hurt Siobhan. He'll disappear and we'll never get him."

"And if you go in alone and things go sideways, you're dead. At least my way you've got a chance."

We sat there. Two people who'd worked together a lifetime ago. Who kept saving each other despite knowing better.

"I need you to trust me," she said. "Can you do that?"

Could I?

"Yeah. I can trust you."

"Good. Then here's the plan. You do the delivery exactly like Emmett wants. We stay invisible. If it goes smooth, you complete it. Bring back the money. Maintain your cover. If it goes bad, if there's violence or danger, we move in. Extract you. Blow the whole thing up if we have to."

"What about the evidence? The case?"

"We've got enough. Your recordings. The documented deliveries. The recruitment tactics. If we have to burn the cover to save your life, we burn it."

"And Siobhan?"

"If we raid, we get her out. Deprogram her. Get her help. It won't be what she wants. But she'll be alive."

It was a plan. Not a great one. But better than going in alone.

"Okay," I said. "I'll wear the wire. Document everything. Try to get Emmett on record about the operation. The bigger the evidence, the stronger the case."

"Exactly. But Blair? Your priority is staying alive. Not getting evidence. Not saving Siobhan. Not proving anything to anyone. Just staying alive. Can you commit to that?"

"I'll try."

"Not good enough. I need you to promise. Actually promise. That if things go bad, you'll signal us. You'll let us pull you out."

I looked at her. Saw the fear underneath the anger. Saw how much she cared despite the professional distance.

"I promise," I said. "If things go bad, I'll signal."

"How?"

"I'll text you a period. Just a period. That's the signal. You see that, you come in fast."

"Okay. I'll have my phone on me all night. Watching."

She reached across the table. Took my hand. Human contact. Rare from her.

"Don't die on me, Blair. I've lost enough partners."

"You never lost me. I was always right here. Being an idiot."

"Same thing."

She let go. Pulled out her phone. Made a call.

"It's me. I need a team for tonight. Plainclothes. Unmarked cars. High-risk surveillance. Venice area... No, I can't explain yet... Just trust me... Okay. Thanks."

She hung up.

"Team's set. We'll have three units in the area. Far enough away to stay invisible. Close enough to move fast."

"Thank you."

"Don't thank me. Just don't fuck this up."

I finished my coffee. Checked the time. Had been gone over an hour. Needed to get back before Emmett sent people looking.

"I have to go. Cole's probably freaking out."

"One more thing." She pulled out a small device. Looked like a button. "New wire. Smaller. Better. Harder to detect. Put this in your jacket. It'll record and stream everything."

I took it. Palmed it.

"And this." She handed me a small card. Phone number written on it. "Burner phone. Clean. If you need to reach me and can't use your regular phone, call this number. It's not logged anywhere. Not connected to anything. Just between us."

I put the card in my pocket.

"See you on the other side," she said.

"Yeah."

I left the diner. Caught the bus back to Venice.

Thought about Dashiell Hammett. About Continental Op walking into traps knowing they were traps. About doing the job because that's what you do. About honor among thieves and cops and everyone in between.

I was walking into a trap tonight.

But at least I wasn't walking alone.

Got back to the house. Cole was waiting. Looking furious.

"Where the fuck did you go?"

"Coffee shop. Then walked the beach. Like I said."

"I lost you."

"That's on you. I went where I said I'd go."

He grabbed my arm. Hard. "You pull that shit again, I put you down. Understand?"

"Understood."

He let go. But the message was clear. I was on a short leash.

Emmett appeared. "Everything okay?"

"Fine," Cole said. "He went for coffee. Came back."

"Good." Emmett turned to me. "Rest this afternoon. Eat. Prepare. Tonight's important. Prove yourself tonight, and you're family for real. Fuck it up, and you're gone. One way or another."

"I'll be ready."

The afternoon crawled. I stayed in my room. Activated the new wire Torres gave me. Hid it in my jacket lining.

Checked the gun Emmett gave me. Loaded. Safety on. A nine millimeter. Standard street weapon.

Wondered if I'd have to use it.

Wondered if I could.

Jason came in. Sat on his sleeping bag. Looked at me.

"You scared?" he asked.

"Yeah."

"Me too. When I did my first big delivery. Thought I'd fuck it up. Get killed. But I didn't. You won't either."

"Thanks."

"Emmett's testing you. But he wouldn't send you if he didn't think you could do it. He sees something in you. Same as he saw in all of us."

"What does he see?"

"Someone worth saving. Someone who needs purpose. Someone who'll fight for the family."

I wondered if that was true.

Wondered if Emmett saw anything beyond a tool to use and discard.

Wondered if it mattered.

Evening came.

Cole briefed me on the route. The address. The dealers. What to expect.

"They're not like the usual contacts," he said. "These guys are serious. Violent. Unpredictable. Don't make sudden moves. Don't try to negotiate. Just deliver. Collect. Leave."

"Got it."

"And Pete? If this goes wrong, if cops show up, if anything feels off—you run. Don't try to be a hero. Just run. Emmett will understand."

"Okay."

At ten-thirty, Emmett gave me the product. Black duffel. Heavy. Had to be ten kilos. Half a million wholesale.

"Address is in your pocket," he said. "Phone number too. Call when you're done. We'll pick you up."

"What if something goes wrong?"

"Then we never see you again. And you better hope the cops get you before we do."

He smiled. But his eyes were dead serious.

"Don't let me down, Pete. I'm starting to believe in you."

I took the duffel. Got in the van Cole had prepared. Keys in the ignition.

Sat there for a moment. Gun in my waistband. Wire in my jacket. Half a million in drugs on the seat beside me.

Texted Torres: *Leaving now. Address is 2847 East 95th St. Target time 11:15.*

Her response: *We're ready. Stay safe.*

I started the van.

Drove into the night.

Toward the delivery. Toward the test. Toward whatever waited at the end.

Twenty-four days left in Emmett's deal.

Might not make it through tonight.

But I was going anyway.

Because that's what you do when you've got nothing left to lose.

You drive toward the danger.

And hope you're good enough to survive it.

# Chapter 19: The Witness

**The address was in Watts.**

Deep south LA. The kind of neighborhood where street lights stay broken and sirens are background noise. Where people mind their business because minding other people's business gets you killed.

I drove slow. Checking mirrors. Looking for Torres's team. Didn't see them. Which meant they were good at their jobs. Or not there at all.

Had to trust they were there.

Had to trust something.

2847 East 95th Street was a house set back from the road. Chain-link fence. Bars on windows. Dogs barking somewhere in the yard. Two cars in the driveway. Both expensive. Both out of place in this neighborhood.

I pulled up. Parked on the street. Sat there for a moment.

The wire in my jacket was recording. The gun in my waistband was loaded. The duffel bag beside me held enough cocaine to put me away for twenty years.

"Same as everyone. Lost everything. Emmett gave me purpose."

"Purpose." He said it like the word tasted bad. "You believe that shit? The family bullshit? The community?"

"I believe in staying alive."

That he liked. Smiled for real this time.

"Smart. Most of Emmett's people are true believers. Idiots who think they're doing God's work. But you? You got eyes open. I can tell."

He stood. Walked to a safe in the corner. Opened it. Pulled out stacks of cash.

"Half a million. Count it if you want."

"I trust you."

"No you don't. But you're in a hurry. Smart."

He loaded the cash into the now-empty duffel. Zipped it. Handed it to me.

"Tell Emmett we need more next week. Double this amount. Can he handle that?"

"I'll ask."

"You do that." He gestured to his men. "Walk him out. Make sure he gets to his car safe. Neighborhood's dangerous at night."

They walked me out. All four of them. Surrounded me like an honor guard for a prisoner.

Got to the van. Opened the door. Put the duffel on the seat.

One of them grabbed my arm.

"Hold up. Something I need to know."

"What?"

"You ever been a cop?"

My heart stopped. Kept my face neutral.

"No. Why?"

"Because you move like one. Stand like one. Ask questions like one."

"I worked security. Before I lost my job. Same training."

He stared at me. Looking for the lie.

The other men were tense now. Hands near weapons. Ready.

This was the moment. The edge of the blade. One wrong word and I was dead.

"Security," he repeated. "What kind?"

"Private. Rich people who wanted poor people to protect them from other poor people. Usual bullshit."

He let go of my arm. Stepped back.

"Get out of here. Tell Emmett to send Cole next time. I don't trust new faces."

I got in the van. Started the engine. Drove away slow. Watching the mirrors.

They stood in the street. Watching until I turned the corner.

I drove three blocks. Pulled over. Sat there shaking.

The wire had recorded everything. The transaction. The conversation. The half-million in cash sitting beside me.

Texted Torres: *Deal done. Heading back.*

Her response: *Good. We followed the whole thing. Got eyes on those guys now. Good work.*

I sat there for another minute. Let the adrenaline settle. Let my hands stop shaking.

Thought about what the dealer said. About moving like a cop. About how close I'd come to being exposed.

Started driving back to Venice.

Thought about what came next. Delivering the cash to Emmett. Proving myself. Staying embedded.

Twenty-four more days of this.

If I survived.

My phone rang. Not the burner. The surveillance phone Torres gave me.

I answered.

"Blair. It's me." Torres. "Listen. Those guys you just met? We ran the house. It's connected to a major trafficking organization. The cash you're carrying? It's evidence in about six open cases. You did good. Really good."

"Didn't feel good."

"It never does. But you got what we needed. Proof of Emmett's connection to major dealers. Proof of the money flow. This is the link we've been looking for."

"What now?"

"Now you deliver the cash to Emmett. Maintain cover. Keep documenting. We're close, Blair. Few more days and we'll have enough to move."

"Few more days."

"Can you hold out?"

"Don't have much choice."

"You've always got a choice. But yeah, staying in is the smart play. Just be careful. If they suspected you tonight, they'll keep watching."

"I know."

"Call me when you're back safe."

"Will do."

She hung up.

I drove through LA at midnight. The city dark and vast and full of people doing things they shouldn't. Selling and buying and hurting and surviving.

I was one of them now.

Had been for a while.

The line between cop and criminal was gone. Between investigator and participant. Between Peter Blair and Pete the follower.

I was just another person carrying half a million in blood money through the city. Trying to stay alive. Trying to finish a job. Trying to mean something.

Walter Mosley wrote about Easy Rawlins navigating between worlds. Black and white. Legal and illegal. Trying to do right in a world that made right impossible.

I understood Easy now.

Understood the compromises. The moral gray. The way you became what you fought just to survive it.

Got back to Venice at twelve-thirty.

The house was dark except for Emmett's office. Light on. Waiting.

I walked in with the duffel.

Emmett was there. Cole beside him. Both watching me like I was evidence that needed examination.

I put the duffel on the desk. Unzipped it. Showed them the cash.

Emmett smiled. "Half a million. On time. No problems."

"No problems."

"How were the dealers?"

"Professional. Dangerous. One of them asked about doubling next week's order."

"Interesting. We'll consider it." He started counting the money. Fast. Practiced. "How'd they treat you?"

"Suspicious. One thought I might be a cop. But I played it right. Convinced him."

"Good. That's the thing about this work. Everyone's suspicious. Everyone's looking for the rat. You have to be comfortable with suspicion. Embrace it even."

He finished counting. All there.

"You did well tonight, Pete. Proved yourself. Showed you can handle pressure. That matters."

"Thanks."

"But." He looked at me. Hard. "You still smell like whiskey. From last night. I can tell. You've been drinking."

No point denying it.

"Yeah. I had a slip. Stressed about the arrest. About proving myself. About all of it."

"We don't allow drinking in the family. You know that."

"I know."

"But we also understand slips. Understand pressure. That's why we have each other. To help when we're weak."

He came around the desk.

Put his hand on my shoulder.

"You're doing well, Pete. Really well. Keep it up and Siobhan walks in twenty-four days. Keep it up and you become real family. Not just temporary help. Real."

"That the goal?"

"Isn't it? Finding family? Finding purpose? That's what you said you wanted."

"Yeah. It is."

"Good. Now get some rest. Tomorrow you've got more work. Always more work in service of the family."

I left his office. Went upstairs. My room.

Jason and Marcus were asleep.

I lay down.

Pulled out the surveillance phone. Checked the recording. Everything captured. The delivery. The conversation. Emmett's counting the money. All of it.

Texted Torres: *Delivered. Emmett accepted it. Cover maintained.*

Her response: *Good. Rest. Check in tomorrow.*

I deleted the messages. Hid the phone.

Lay there in the dark.

Thought about what Emmett said. About becoming real family. About the goal of finding purpose.

Thought about how good it felt to complete the delivery. To prove myself. To belong.

Thought about how dangerous that feeling was.

Twenty-four days.

Had to last twenty-four more days without losing myself completely.

Without forgetting this was temporary. A role. An investigation.

Without becoming Pete for real.

Sleep didn't come easy.

But eventually it came.

And with it, dreams of belonging to something I'd have to destroy.

Of finding family I'd have to abandon.

Of being someone I wasn't.

But wanted to be.

That scared me more than the dealers.

More than the guns.

More than death.

The fear of wanting to stay.

Of surrendering.

Of choosing the lie over the truth.

Twenty-four days.

Just had to remember who I was for twenty-four more days.

Simple.

Except nothing about this was simple anymore.

Nothing at all.

# Chapter 20: The Plan

**Three days after the delivery, Torres called an emergency meeting.**

I slipped out during morning outreach. Told Rachel I needed to check on some personal business. She trusted me now. Everyone did. The successful delivery had earned credibility.

That was the problem.

Met Torres at a different location this time. Coffee shop in Inglewood. Neutral territory. Anonymous.

She was already there. Laptop open. Files spread across the table. Working mode.

I sat down. Ordered coffee I wouldn't drink.

"We need to move," she said. No greeting. All business.

"Move how?"

"Raid. Within the week. We've got enough evidence. Drug trafficking. Prostitution. Fraud. Conspiracy. Enough charges to put Emmett away for twenty years minimum."

"What about the others? Rachel, Marcus, all the true believers?"

"They'll be processed. Interviewed. Released probably. Unless they were directly involved in crimes. Most of them are victims. We get that."

"What about Siobhan?"

"She gets extracted. Taken to a facility. Deprogrammed. Eventually returned to her father."

I thought about Siobhan. About the conversation we'd had. About how completely she believed.

"She'll fight it. She won't go willingly."

"They never do. But it's for her own good. She's been manipulated. Exploited. She doesn't know what she wants."

"She thinks she does."

"That's the manipulation talking." Torres closed her laptop. Looked at me directly. "The question is: are you ready? Can you hold it together for three more days? Then we move. Then it's over."

Three days.

Not twenty-four. Not the full month I'd promised Emmett.

"What about the deal? I told him I'd stay the full month. That was the arrangement."

"The arrangement was bullshit. He was never going to let Siobhan go. You know that. This was always going to end with a raid. With us taking her by force. The only question was when."

She was right. I'd known it from the beginning.

But part of me had wanted to believe. Wanted to think I could actually complete the deal. Actually save her through patience and commitment.

"Three days," I said. "What's the timing?"

"Friday night. We hit them during evening service. When everyone's gathered. Maximum people present. Minimum chance of anyone running."

"That's also maximum chaos. Maximum chance someone gets hurt."

"We'll have overwhelming force. SWAT. Tactical units. Negotiators. This will be professional. Clean. Nobody needs to get hurt if everyone cooperates."

"And if they don't cooperate? If they think we're attacking their family? If they fight back?"

"Then we deal with it. But that's on them. Not us."

I thought about Rachel. About Marcus. About Jason and all the others who'd welcomed me. Who'd trusted me. Who'd shared their meals and their stories and their hope.

I was going to betray them.

Had been betraying them all along.

"What do you need from me?" I asked.

"Three things. One: keep documenting. Everything. Until the raid. The more evidence, the stronger the case. Two: on Friday, position yourself near Siobhan. When we come in, grab her. Keep her safe. Make sure she doesn't get hurt in the chaos. Three: after it's over, testify. Tell the truth about what you saw. What you experienced. What Emmett did."

"Testify meaning go public. Meaning blow my cover completely."

"Your cover's temporary anyway. It ends Friday. Might as well end it with impact. Your testimony will help convict Emmett. Will help the prosecution."

"And make me a rat. A traitor. Everything I pretended not to be."

"You're not a rat. You're an investigator who did his job. There's a difference."

Maybe. But the people in that house wouldn't see it that way.

"What about protection? After? Emmett's got connections. People outside. If I testify, if my face is public, I'm a target."

"We can offer protective custody. Relocation if necessary. Depends on the threat assessment."

Protective custody. Witness protection. Running for the rest of my life.

All to save a girl who didn't want saving.

"I need to think about it," I said.

"Think fast. Friday's in three days. I need to know you're committed. Need to know you won't back out at the last minute."

"I won't back out."

"Promise me."

"I promise."

She didn't look convinced. "What's going on with you, Blair? You're different. More hesitant. More conflicted. Talk to me."

How to explain it? How to describe the pull of belonging? The temptation of surrender?

"I'm tired," I said finally. "Tired of pretending. Tired of lying. Tired of being two people at once."

"Three more days. Then you can stop pretending. Be yourself again."

"What if I don't remember who that is?"

She reached across the table. Took my hand. Same gesture from weeks ago. Concern and connection.

"You're Peter Blair. Former cop. Private investigator. Recovering alcoholic. Good man underneath all the damage. That's who you are. Don't forget it."

"I'm trying not to."

"Try harder. Because if you lose yourself in there, if you go native, you're no good to anyone. Not to me. Not to Siobhan. Not to yourself."

"I know."

"Do you? Because I'm worried about you. Really worried. You sound like someone who's thinking about staying. About choosing them over us."

Was I? Was that what this was?

"I'm not choosing them. I'm just... I understand them now. Understand why they stay. Why they believe. It's not just manipulation. There's real community there. Real belonging. Real purpose. That's powerful."

"It's also built on lies. On exploitation. On Emmett using vulnerable people for his own ends. Don't romanticize it."

"I'm not romanticizing it. I'm just acknowledging it's complicated."

"It's not complicated. It's criminal. And Friday we shut it down. You're either with me on that or you're not."

She pulled her hand back. All business again.

"I'm with you," I said. "Friday. I'll be ready."

"Good. Now get back before they miss you. Stay low. Stay safe. Don't do anything stupid."

I left the coffee shop.

Caught the bus back to Venice.

Thought about Ross Macdonald. About Lew Archer finding lost people who didn't want to be found. About the morality of saving someone from themselves. About whether rescue and kidnapping were really that different.

Siobhan didn't want rescue. Didn't think she needed saving.

But we were going to save her anyway.

For her own good. For her father. For the principle of the thing.

Whether she liked it or not.

That felt wrong somehow.

But so did leaving her there.

No good options. Just choices that all hurt someone.

Got back to the house mid-afternoon. Rachel was waiting.

"Pete! Where were you? We missed you at lunch."

"Had to handle some personal stuff. Old debts. Needed to close some accounts from my previous life."

"Everything okay?"

"Yeah. Just loose ends."

She smiled. "Good. Because tonight's special. Emmett's holding a big gathering. Inviting people from outside the family. Potential new members. He wants everyone there. Showing our best."

"I'll be there."

"Great! And Pete? I'm really glad you found us. You've been such a positive addition. Everyone says so."

She meant it. Genuine warmth. Genuine acceptance.

I was going to destroy her world in three days.

"Thanks, Rachel. That means a lot."

She walked away. Happy. Purposeful. Completely unaware.

I went to my room. Checked the surveillance equipment. Still recording. Still uploading. Still building the case that would end all this.

Jason was there. Sitting on his sleeping bag. Looking troubled.

"You okay?" I asked.

"Yeah. Just... thinking."

"About what?"

"About what happens if this all falls apart. If Emmett gets arrested. If the family dissolves. Where do we go? What do we do?"

Prophetic question.

"Why would it fall apart?"

"I don't know. Just feels fragile lately. Like we're balanced on something that could tip. You feel it?"

"Feel what?"

"The tension. Emmett's been different. More paranoid. More controlling. Like he's expecting something bad."

He was. He was expecting exactly what was coming.

"He's just being careful," I said. "Protecting the family."

"Maybe." Jason didn't look convinced. "But what if he can't protect us? What if something happens and we're all just... scattered? Back to where we were before?"

"Then we survive. Same as we always have."

"I don't know if I can go back to that. To being alone. To having no purpose. This place saved me. I don't know who I am without it."

I sat down next to him. Two men in a room. Both pretending to be someone they weren't.

"You're more than this place, Jason. You were someone before Emmett. You'll be someone after."

"Will I? Or will I just be a junkie who got clean for a while then relapsed? That's who I was. That's who I'll be again."

"You don't know that."

"Yeah. I do. We all do. That's why we stay. Because out there, we're nothing. In here, we're family. We matter."

He was giving voice to the same thoughts I'd been having. The same fears.

The same temptation to choose the lie because the truth was harder.

"What would you do?" he asked. "If this all ended tomorrow? If you had to leave and go back to your old life?"

"I'd remember what I learned here. The good parts. The community. The purpose. And I'd try to build something real. Something that lasted."

"You think that's possible?"

"I don't know. But I'd try."

He nodded. Seemed to accept that.

"Thanks, Pete. For listening. For being here. You're good people."

"So are you."

He left. Went to help with dinner prep.

I sat there alone.

Thought about what he said. About what happened when this ended. About who I'd be when I wasn't Pete anymore.

Would I go back to being Peter Blair? The failed cop turned mediocre PI?

Or had I changed? Had these weeks embedded in Emmett's family altered something fundamental?

Didn't know.

Couldn't know until Friday.

Until the raid. Until the end.

That night's gathering was bigger than usual. Fifty people. Sixty. Emmett had recruited hard. Brought in potential new members. Showed them the family. The community. The belonging.

I watched him work the crowd. Charismatic. Warm. Genuine seeming.

Watched people respond. Opening up. Trusting. Wanting what he offered.

Watched the machinery of recruitment and manipulation disguised as love.

Siobhan was there. Radiant. Happy. Helping welcome newcomers. Living her purpose.

In three days I'd rip her from this. Tell her it was all lies. Force her into deprogramming whether she wanted it or not.

For her own good.

The phrase made me sick.

After the gathering, Emmett pulled me aside.

"Walk with me."

We walked along the canals.

Just the two of us. Moonlight on water. Venice quiet for once.

"You've done well, Pete. Better than I expected. Better than most."

"Thanks."

"I'm going to be honest with you. When you first came here, I didn't trust you. Thought you might be a plant. A cop. Someone sent to destroy what we built."

My heart rate picked up. Kept my expression neutral.

"And now?"

"Now I think you're genuine. Damaged like the rest of us. Looking for meaning in a meaningless world. I respect that."

"I appreciate the trust."

"Don't appreciate it. Earn it. Every day. That's how family works. Continuous earning. Continuous proving."

"I understand."

He stopped walking. Looked at me.

"Do you? Because I'm about to tell you something. Something I don't tell everyone. And if you betray this confidence, if you use it against me, I'll know. And you'll regret it."

"I'm listening."

"I know you were a cop. I know you arrested my brother. I know he died because of that arrest. I've known from the beginning. That's why I let you in. That's why I tested you. That's why I watched you so carefully."

He knew. Had always known.

"And you still let me stay?"

"Yes. Because I wanted to understand you. Wanted to see if you were worth saving. Wanted to see if you could change. If someone complicit in my brother's death could become someone who helped people instead of hurting them."

"And? What's the verdict?"

"You're changing. I can see it. You came here damaged. Guilty. Self-destructive. Now you're finding purpose. Finding family. Finding redemption. That's beautiful. That's what this is all about."

He put his hand on my shoulder.

"In twenty-one days, Siobhan goes free. Like I promised. But I'm hoping you stay. Not as a temporary member. As real family. As someone who believes. Who helps build what we're creating. Someone who understands that the past doesn't define us. Only our choices now."

He was offering me everything I thought I wanted.

Community. Purpose. Forgiveness. Belonging.

All I had to do was betray Torres. Betray the investigation. Betray everything I'd worked for.

Become Pete for real.

"I need to think about it," I said.

"Think fast. Because Friday I'm making changes. Expanding the operation. Bringing in new leadership. People who've proven themselves. People like you. If you want a place in that future, you need to commit. Fully. No more half measures."

"I'll think about it."

"Good. Think hard. Because this is a one-time offer. Choose us or choose out. But choose."

We walked back to the house in silence.

My mind racing.

Friday. Emmett was planning expansions on the same day Torres was planning the raid.

Either I stopped the expansion by letting the raid happen.

Or I warned Emmett. Saved the family. Became the traitor to the law instead of the family.

Three days to decide.

Three days to choose who I was.

Three days to figure out which betrayal I could live with.

I went to my room.

Texted Torres: *Emmett knows I was a cop. Knows about his brother. Has known all along. Offering me real membership. Wants answer by Friday.*

Her response came fast: *Jesus. Are you safe?*

*For now. He thinks I'm changing. Thinks I'm becoming one of them.*

*Are you?*

Was I?

*Don't know. Call you tomorrow. Need to think.*

*Don't think too long. We move Friday regardless. Be ready.*

I deleted the messages.

Lay down. Stared at the ceiling.

Thought about choices. About betrayals. About the difference between rescue and destruction.

Thought about Siobhan. About the people who trusted me. About the evidence I'd gathered.

Thought about Emmett's offer. About belonging. About redemption through surrender.

Thought about Peter Blair. About who he was. About whether he still existed.

Three days.

Everything would be decided in three days.

And I still didn't know which side I'd choose when the moment came.

That terrified me more than anything.

Because it should have been simple.

Should have been obvious.

But it wasn't.

Not anymore.

# Chapter 21: Into the House

**Friday came too fast.**

I woke up knowing what I had to do.

Didn't mean I liked it.

The house was busy all day. Preparations for the evening gathering. Emmett's expansion plans. New members coming. Big announcements planned.

He found me at breakfast.

"Tonight's important, Pete. After the gathering, I'm making my offer official. Leadership position. Real family. I need your answer."

"You'll have it tonight."

"Good. I'm hoping it's yes. You've proven yourself. Shown growth. Shown commitment. We need people like you."

He walked away. Confident. Sure I'd choose him.

Maybe he was right to be.

I spent the day in a fog. Going through motions. Helping set up. Avoiding Rachel's cheerful energy. Avoiding Jason's hopeful questions.

Avoiding thinking about what came next.

At four p.m., I slipped out. Told Cole I needed air. He let me go. Trusted me now.

Everyone trusted me.

Called Torres from a pay phone.

"It's me. Tonight's still on?"

"Yes. We hit them at seven-thirty. During the gathering. You ready?"

Was I?

"Yeah. I'm ready."

"Where will Siobhan be?"

"Front of the gathering. She always sits there. I'll position myself near her. When you come in, I'll grab her. Keep her safe."

"Good. And Blair? When this starts, it's going to be chaos. People will panic. Run. Fight maybe. You keep your head down. Protect the girl. Let us handle the rest."

"Okay."

"And after... you'll testify? You'll do what needs doing?"

"Yeah. I'll testify."

She was quiet for a moment. "You don't sound certain."

"I'm certain. Just... tired. Ready for it to be over."

"It will be. After tonight. You can go back to being yourself. Leave Pete behind."

"Right."

"Blair. You know this is the right thing. You know that."

Did I?

"Yeah. I know."

"Then stay strong. Three more hours. Then it's done."

I hung up. Stood there in the fading afternoon light.

Thought about calling Lonnie. Telling him what I was about to do. Getting absolution or wisdom or something.

Didn't call.

Some things you have to do alone.

Walked back to the house. The gathering was forming. People arriving. Sixty. Seventy. More than usual.

Emmett had pulled out all the stops. Food. Music. The full community experience.

Recruitment event disguised as worship.

Or worship event disguised as recruitment.

Hard to tell the difference anymore.

I found Siobhan in the kitchen. She was helping prepare food. Radiant. In her element.

"Pete! Can you help carry these platters out?"

"Sure."

We worked together. Carrying food to the gathering space. Setting up.

"Big night," she said.

"Yeah. Emmett's got plans."

"He always does. That's what makes him amazing. Always thinking ahead. Always building something bigger."

"You really believe in him."

"Of course. He saved my life. Gave me purpose. How could I not believe?"

"And you're happy? Really happy?"

She stopped. Looked at me. "Why are you asking?"

"Just curious. Making sure you're where you want to be."

"I'm exactly where I want to be. This is my family now. My real family. The only one that matters."

She meant it. Every word.

In ninety minutes, I'd rip that away from her.

Seven o'clock. The gathering began.

Emmett took center stage. Preaching. Welcoming. Building energy.

The crowd responded. Engaged. Eager.

I sat near the front. Siobhan three feet away. Positioned exactly where I told Torres I'd be.

My phone was in my pocket. Surveillance equipment recording. Wire active.

Everything documented. Everything ready.

Emmett spoke about family. About community. About the future they were building together.

Spoke about expansion. About new opportunities. About leadership positions for those who'd proven themselves.

Looked at me when he said it. Direct eye contact.

Waiting for my answer.

I nodded. Small gesture. Enough.

He smiled. Thought I'd chosen him.

Maybe I had.

Seven-twenty. Ten minutes until the raid.

My heart was pounding. Hands sweating.

Checked my phone. No messages from Torres. Everything on schedule.

Seven-twenty-five.

Emmett was reaching the climax of his sermon. The emotional peak. Everyone rapt. Attentive.

"We are family," he said. "We are chosen. We are free. And tonight we welcome new brothers and sisters. Tonight we expand our love. Tonight we—"

The doors burst open.

"Police! Everyone down! Down on the ground now!"

SWAT flooded in. Fifteen officers. Twenty. Full tactical gear. Weapons drawn.

Chaos erupted.

People screaming. Running. Panic.

Emmett stood frozen. Shocked. Betrayed looking.

I grabbed Siobhan. Pulled her down. Covered her with my body.

"Stay down! Don't move!"

She fought me. "What's happening? What's—"

"Police raid. Just stay down. You're safe."

Officers moving through the crowd. Separating people. Identifying targets.

Cole and Brandon tried to run. Tackled immediately. Cuffed.

Rachel was crying. Confused. Scared.

Marcus was on his knees. Hands behind his head. Complying.

Jason was curled in a ball. Protecting himself. Terrified.

Torres entered. In plainclothes but with a badge visible. Commanding.

She found me. Found Siobhan.

"Blair. You good?"

"Yeah. She's safe."

Siobhan looked at me. Confused. "Blair? Your name's Pete."

"No. It's not."

Understanding dawned. Horror. Betrayal.

"You're a cop."

"Private investigator. Working for your father."

She tried to pull away. Torres grabbed her arm.

"Miss Fury. You're safe now. We're getting you out."

"I don't want out! This is my home! These are my people!"

"These people exploited you. Manipulated you. You're coming with us."

Two female officers moved in. Helped Torres restrain Siobhan. She fought. Screamed. Called for Emmett.

Emmett was on his knees now. Officers surrounding him. Reading rights.

He looked at me. Across the chaos. Across the betrayed gathering.

Our eyes met.

He smiled. Sad smile. Knowing.

Mouthed words: *I knew.*

Had he? Had he known all along this was coming?

Or was he just claiming knowledge after the fact?

Didn't matter now.

Torres had Siobhan. Officers were processing everyone. Separating victims from perpetrators. Documenting evidence.

The gathering was over.

The family was broken.

And I was the one who broke it.

Rachel saw me standing. Saw Torres. Saw the badge. Understood.

"Pete? You... you did this?"

I couldn't look at her.

"I'm sorry."

"You're sorry? You destroyed us! We trusted you! We loved you!"

She collapsed. Crying. Other members gathering around her. Comforting. United in betrayal.

Marcus approached me. Slow. Deliberate. Officers tense. Ready to intervene.

"You were never one of us," he said. "Never family. Just a spy. A liar."

"I was trying to help."

"Help? You call this help? Destroying the only place we belonged? The only purpose we had?"

He turned away. Joined the others.

Jason wouldn't even look at me. Just sat there. Devastated. Lost.

Torres pulled me aside.

"You did good. We got Emmett. Got his security guys. Got evidence of everything. This is a solid case."

"Great."

"You don't sound happy."

"I'm not."

"You saved these people, Blair. Saved them from exploitation. From manipulation. They'll understand eventually."

"Will they?"

She didn't answer.

Officers were loading Emmett into a patrol car. Cole and Brandon already gone.

The crowd was being processed. Names taken. Statements given. Released if they weren't directly involved in crimes.

Which was most of them.

Most of them were just lost people who found belonging in the wrong place.

Torres had Siobhan in a car. Taking her to a facility. For evaluation. For deprogramming.

For her own good.

Siobhan was still fighting. Still screaming. Still believing.

I watched the car drive away.

Thought about Declan. About how I'd call him. Tell him I found his daughter. Tell him she was safe.

Tell him she hated me now. Hated him. Hated everyone who'd "rescued" her.

Tell him this was what success looked like.

The house was empty now. Everyone gone. Just officers processing evidence. Documenting the scene.

Torres found me standing in the main room. The place where we'd eaten meals together. Shared stories. Built community.

"We need your statement," she said. "Full debrief. Everything you saw. Everything you experienced."

"Okay."

"And Blair? Thank you. I know this wasn't easy. But you did the right thing."

Had I?

"Yeah. The right thing."

She left me there.

I stood alone in the empty house.

Thought about Pete. About the person I'd pretended to be. About the person I'd almost become.

Thought about the family I'd betrayed. About the trust I'd destroyed. About the community I'd shattered.

Thought about whether any of it mattered. Whether saving Siobhan from herself justified destroying everyone else's refuge.

My phone buzzed. Text from Declan.

*Torres called. Said you found her. Said she's safe. Thank you. Thank you so much.*

I didn't respond.

Couldn't tell him the truth. That his daughter was safe but broken. Rescued but resentful. Alive but hating everyone who'd saved her.

Couldn't tell him I'd succeeded in the worst possible way.

Won the case. Lost everything else.

An officer approached. "Sir? We need you to come downtown. Give your statement. Process the evidence."

"Yeah. Okay."

I followed him out. Into the Venice night.

The boardwalk was still selling itself. Tourists still walking. Performers still performing.

Like nothing had happened.

Like a family hadn't just been destroyed three blocks away.

I got in Torres's car. She drove us to the station.

Neither of us spoke.

What was there to say?

Raymond Chandler wrote that down these mean streets a man must go who is not himself mean. Who is neither tarnished nor afraid.

I'd gone down the mean streets.

But I was tarnished now.

Tarnished by the lies I'd told. The trust I'd betrayed. The family I'd destroyed.

Tarnished by doing the right thing in the wrong way.

Or the wrong thing in the right way.

Couldn't tell anymore.

At the station, I gave my statement. Twelve hours of testimony. Everything I'd seen. Everything I'd done. Everything I'd documented.

They had enough to convict Emmett. Enough to shut down the operation. Enough to prosecute everyone involved.

Success.

It felt like failure.

Dawn came. They let me go. Said I could go home. Get rest. They'd be in touch about trial testimony.

Torres drove me to my apartment. Pulled up outside.

"You okay?" she asked.

"No."

"You will be. Give it time."

"Time doesn't fix this."

"Maybe not. But it helps."

I got out. Stood there.

"Blair. What you did in there... it mattered. You saved people. You stopped a criminal operation. You got a dangerous man off the streets. That matters."

"To who?"

"To everyone. To the system. To justice. To the people who'll never get exploited by Emmett now."

"What about the people who just lost the only family they had? What about them?"

She didn't have an answer.

I walked to my apartment. Unlocked the door. Went inside.

The space was the same. Books and coffee maker and Murphy bed.

But I was different.

Changed by weeks of being someone else. Changed by the betrayal. Changed by the success that felt like failure.

Sat down. Stared at nothing.

My phone rang. Lonnie.

I answered.

"You're alive," he said.

"Yeah."

"Torres called. Told me what happened. Told me you survived. Told me you did good."

"Did I?"

"You did what you set out to do. Found the girl. Stopped the operation. Stayed sober through most of it."

"Most of it."

"Relapse happens. You got back up. That's what matters."

"I destroyed people's lives, Lonnie. Good people who were just looking for belonging."

"They were being exploited. You freed them."

"They don't see it that way."

"They will. Eventually. When they've had time. When they've healed. They'll understand you saved them."

"You really believe that?"

"I have to. Otherwise nothing we do matters."

We sat there. Connected by phone. Connected by damage. Connected by the need to believe suffering means something.

"What now?" I asked.

"Now you rest. Now you heal. Now you figure out who Peter Blair is when he's not pretending to be someone else."

"What if I don't know anymore?"

"Then you find out. One day at a time. Same as recovery. Same as everything."

"Yeah."

"Come to a meeting tomorrow. See some friendly faces. Remember you're not alone."

"Okay."

"And Blair? I'm proud of you. For what it's worth. You did something hard. Something necessary. Something right. Even if it doesn't feel that way."

"Thanks, Lonnie."

"Anytime."

He hung up.

I sat there.

Alone in my apartment.

Peter Blair again.

Not Pete. Not anyone else. Just me.

Whoever that was.

The sun came up. Light through my window.

Venice Beach was out there. Still selling itself. Still running cons. Still breaking hearts.

I'd stopped one small piece of it.

Destroyed a family to save a girl.

Won and lost at the same time.

That was noir, I guess.

That was Los Angeles.

That was life.

I made coffee. Strong and black.

Sat at my window. Watched the city wake up.

Wondered if Siobhan would forgive me.

Wondered if Rachel or Marcus or Jason would understand someday.

Wondered if I'd ever forgive myself.

Didn't have answers.

Just coffee and dawn and the weight of necessary betrayals.

Twenty-one days left in the deal I'd made with Emmett.

Didn't matter now.

The deal was broken.
The family was broken.
Everything was broken.
But Siobhan was alive.
And that would have to be enough.

# Chapter 22: The Reckoning

**Two weeks after the raid, I met Declan Fury at a diner in Koreatown.**

Same place we'd both gone to AA meetings. Neutral ground. Memory-soaked.

He was already there when I arrived. Looked older. Worn. Relief and grief fighting on his face.

I sat across from him.

"Blair."

"Declan."

The waitress came. Coffee for both. We didn't order food. This wasn't that kind of meeting.

"I saw her yesterday," he said. "At the facility. They're letting me visit twice a week."

"How is she?"

"Angry. Confused. Won't talk to me. Won't talk to anyone really. The counselors say it's normal. Say she's been through trauma. Needs time."

"Yeah."

"She asked about you."

My stomach tightened. "What did she ask?"

"If I knew. If I hired you. If the whole thing was my idea." He looked at me. "I told her the truth. That I hired you to find her. To make sure she was safe. That I was worried."

"What did she say?"

"She said I destroyed the only family she ever had. Said I'm selfish. Said I never cared about what she wanted. Just what I wanted." His voice cracked. "She's not wrong."

"You did what any father would do."

"Did I? Or did I do what a guilty father does? Try to fix things too late? Control her life because I couldn't control my own?"

Questions I'd been asking myself. Questions without good answers.

"You paid me to find her. I found her. That's all this was supposed to be."

"But it wasn't, was it? It became something else. You lived with them. Became one of them. Betrayed them. For me. For her. For what?"

For what?

"I don't know anymore."

He drank his coffee. Hands shaking slightly. Eight years sober but still damaged. Still broken.

"The counselors say she'll come around eventually. Say once she processes the manipulation, once she understands Emmett was using her, she'll see we saved her. But I don't think that's true."

"Why not?"

"Because part of what she had there was real. The community. The belonging. The purpose. Those weren't lies. Those were real things built on a foundation of lies. And we destroyed all of it. The lies and the truth together."

He understood. Better than I thought he would.

"I owe you money," he said. "The rest of the payment. For finishing the job."

He pulled out an envelope. Put it on the table.

I didn't touch it.

"Keep it. I didn't finish the job. I destroyed it."

"You found her. Got her out. That's what I hired you for."

"I found her. But I didn't get her out. The cops did. And she didn't want getting out. That's not success. That's failure dressed up as rescue."

"Take the money, Blair. You earned it. You did more than I had any right to ask."

I took the envelope. Didn't open it.

"What happens now?" I asked. "With Siobhan?"

"Thirty days in the facility. Mandatory evaluation. Then she's free to go. She's an adult. Can't force her to stay. Can't force her to do anything."

"What if she goes back? Finds what's left of the family? Tries to rebuild?"

"Then I'll have to accept it. Let her make her own choices. Even bad ones. Especially bad ones. That's what the counselors say. That's what recovery teaches. You can't save people from themselves."

Same thing Lonnie told me. Same thing Torres said. Same thing everyone kept saying.

But nobody believed it. Not really.

We all kept trying to save people anyway.

"I'm sorry," I said. "For how this turned out. For the way she hates you now. For all of it."

"Don't be. You did what I asked. The consequences are on me. I hired you. I set this in motion. I destroyed my relationship with my daughter to save her from something she didn't want saving from." He smiled. Bitter. "That's very on-brand for me. The Fury way. Destroy everything with good intentions."

"That's not—"

"It is. You know it is. We're the same, Blair. Both of us trying to fix broken things with broken tools. Both of us making everything worse while trying to make it better."

He stood. Dropped cash on the table.

"Thank you. Genuinely. For trying. For caring enough to try. That's more than most people would do."

"I'm not sure it was enough."

"It never is. But we do it anyway. That's the human condition, right? Trying despite knowing we'll fail. Caring despite knowing it'll hurt."

He walked out.

I sat there with my coffee and my envelope of blood money.

Thought about success and failure. About the difference between them.

Couldn't find one.

Three days later, Torres called. Asked me to meet her at the station. Said there was something I needed to see.

I went. She led me to an interview room.

Emmett was inside. Sitting at the table. Handcuffs. Orange jumpsuit. But somehow still composed. Still in control.

"What's this?" I asked Torres.

"He asked to see you. Said he had something to say. I thought you might want to hear it."

"I don't."

"Blair. Listen to him. Then decide."

She left. Closed the door. Left me alone with the man I'd destroyed.

We sat there. On opposite sides of the table. On opposite sides of everything.

"Pete," he said. Then corrected himself. "Blair. Sorry. Force of habit."

"What do you want?"

"To talk. To understand. To get answers before I go away for twenty years."

"What answers?"

"Why? Why did you really do it? Was it just the money? Just the job? Just because Declan asked you to?"

I thought about lying. Thought about giving him a simple answer.

Gave him the truth instead.

"At first, yeah. Just the job. Just the money. But then... then it became something else."

"What?"

"Guilt. About your brother. About the arrest. About the system that killed him. I wanted to make something right. Thought if I could save Siobhan, if I could stop you, maybe it would balance the scales."

"Did it?"

"No. Nothing balances. It just adds more weight."

He nodded. Understanding.

"I knew from the beginning," he said. "Knew who you were. Knew why you came. Knew about Declan hiring you. I let you in anyway."

"Why?"

"Because I wanted to see if you'd change. Wanted to see if the man who arrested my brother could become the man who understood why I built what I built. Wanted to see if you were capable of growth."

"And?"

"You were. You did. I saw it. Saw you becoming Pete. Saw you finding purpose. Saw you understanding what we offered. You were changing, Blair. Really changing. You felt it, didn't you? The pull of belonging?"

"Yeah. I felt it."

"And you chose to destroy it anyway. Chose law over family. Chose your old identity over your new one. Why?"

Because Torres was waiting. Because Siobhan needed saving. Because it was my job.

Because I was afraid of what I'd become if I stayed.

"Because it was built on lies," I said. "Because you were exploiting people. Because the good things you did didn't excuse the bad things."

"Who decides that? You? The system? The same system that killed my brother? The same system that abandons homeless people? That criminalizes poverty? That forces people into choosing between survival and morality?"

"You had other choices."

"Did I? After they killed David? After they dismissed my complaints? After they told me his death didn't matter? What choices did I have except to build something outside their system?"

"You could have built it clean. Could have helped people without exploiting them."

"Could I? You think people donate to help the homeless?

You think the city funds effective programs? The only way to build anything lasting is to fund it yourself. And the only way to fund it is through business. Sometimes that business is ugly. Sometimes it's illegal. But it feeds people. It houses people. It gives them purpose."

He leaned forward.

"You lived it, Blair. You saw it. The family was real. The community was real. The purpose was real. Yes, I sold drugs. Yes, I had women working. Yes, I took money. But I also fed people. Sheltered people. Gave them something to live for. That's more than the city does. More than the cops do. More than you did before you became Pete."

He was right. About all of it.

And wrong. About all of it.

Both true at once.

"You killed it," he continued. "Destroyed the only home sixty people had. Scattered them back to the streets. Back to drugs and despair and hopelessness. For what? To save one girl who didn't want saving? To put me in prison? To prove you're better than me?"

"I'm not better than you."

"No. You're worse. Because you understand what you destroyed. You felt it. You lived it. You know what you took from them. And you did it anyway. That's not justice. That's cruelty."

His words hit like fists. True and terrible.

"I'm sorry," I said. "About your brother. About what happened. About the system failing him."

"Don't apologize. Apologies don't resurrect the dead. Don't undo the damage. Don't change anything."

"Then what do you want from me?"

"I want you to carry it. The weight of what you did. The knowledge of what you destroyed. I want you to remember their faces when you betrayed them. Want you to hear Rachel crying. Want you to see Jason's devastation. Want you to feel what you took from them every time you look in the mirror."

"I already do."

"Good. Then we're even. You took my brother. I made you take your own soul. We're both guilty. We're both damaged. We're both destroying people while trying to save them."

He stood. Called for the guard.

Before he left, he turned back.

"One more thing. Siobhan. She'll never forgive you. Never forgive her father. She'll carry the loss of the family for the rest of her life. You did that. You and Declan. So when she kills herself in five years because she never finds that belonging again, when she overdoses or jumps or just fades away from sadness—that's on you. Remember that."

The guard took him away.

I sat there alone.

Thought about James Lee Burke. About Dave Robicheaux carrying guilt like stones in his pockets. About good men doing bad things and bad men doing good things and how none of it mattered because suffering was universal and justice was fiction.

Emmett was right.

I'd carry this forever.

Would remember Rachel's tears. Jason's devastation. Marcus's betrayal. Siobhan's hatred.

Would remember the community I destroyed.

The family I scattered.

The purpose I stole.

All to save one person who didn't want saving.

All to prove I could still do something right.

All for nothing.

Torres found me in the interview room twenty minutes later.

"You okay?"

"No."

"What did he say?"

"The truth. That I destroyed something real to save something broken. That I'm no better than him. That I'll carry this forever."

"He's manipulating you. Making you doubt. That's what he does."

"Is it? Or is he just telling me things I already know but don't want to admit?"

She sat down. Across from me. Where Emmett had been.

"You did the right thing," she said. "I know it doesn't feel that way. I know it cost you. But you stopped a criminal operation. You saved people from exploitation. That matters."

"Does it?"

"Yes. It does. And someday you'll believe that again."

"When?"

"I don't know. But I'll be here when you do. That's what partners are for."

"I wasn't your partner."

"You are now."

She stood. Offered her hand. Helped me up.

"Come on. Let's get you out of here. Get you home. Get you to a meeting."

We walked out together. Into the LA afternoon.

The city indifferent as always. Moving forward. Not caring about small tragedies or moral victories or the weight broken men carried.

"Torres," I said. "Thank you. For everything. For backing me. For believing in me. For pulling me out when I couldn't pull myself."

"Anytime. That's what we do. We pull each other out. We survive together. We try to do better tomorrow than we did today."

"And if tomorrow's worse?"

"Then we survive that too."

We got to my car. She hesitated.

"Blair. I need to tell you something."

"What?"

"Rachel. From the family. She tried to kill herself two days ago. Overdose. They found her in time. She's alive. But barely."

The ground shifted.

"Does she... is she okay?"

"Physically, yeah. Mentally, no. She lost everything. Her purpose. Her family. Her reason to live. She's in psychiatric hold now. Seventy-two hours. Then they'll evaluate."

"Jesus Christ."

"It's not your fault."

"Isn't it? I destroyed her world. I took the only thing that kept her alive."

"Emmett took it. When he built it on lies. When he made them dependent. When he exploited their vulnerability. You just exposed it."

"Same result."

"Different cause." She put her hand on my shoulder. "You can't carry everyone's pain, Blair. Can't make yourself responsible for every consequence. You'll drown."

"Maybe I should."

"Maybe. But I'd rather you didn't. World needs good investigators. Good men. Even broken ones. Especially broken ones."

She walked to her car. Drove away.

I stood there in the parking lot.

Thought about Rachel. About her kindness. Her genuine belief. Her trust.

Thought about destroying her.

Thought about all the ways I'd failed while succeeding.

All the ways I'd won while losing.

Drove home through traffic.

Made coffee.

Sat at my window.

Watched Venice Beach sell itself.

Tomorrow I'd call Lonnie. Go to a meeting. Try to rebuild some version of Peter Blair that could live with what he'd done.

Tomorrow I'd try to believe Torres. That I'd done the right thing. That it mattered.

Tomorrow.

But today I just sat there.

Carrying stones.

Drowning slowly.

Surviving despite everything.

Because that's what you do.

You survive.

Even when you don't want to.

Even when surviving feels like punishment.

Even when you've destroyed everything you touched while trying to save it.

You survive.

And hope that's enough.

It had to be.

Nothing else was left.

# Chapter 23: After

**Six weeks later.**

I was in my office when Declan walked in.

Didn't knock. Just walked in like he owned the place. Maybe he did. His money had paid for most of my rent the last two months.

"Blair."

"Declan."

He sat in the client chair. It still wobbled. Some things never changed.

"She got out yesterday. The facility. Thirty days served. They released her."

"Where'd she go?"

"Don't know. She walked out. Didn't tell me. Didn't tell the counselors. Just left."

"You try calling?"

"She blocked my number. Week two." He looked at me. Older somehow. More gray. More tired. "I hired you to find her. Maybe I need to do it again."

"No."

"No?"

"No. She's an adult. She left on her purpose. She doesn't want to be found. Not by you. Not by me. Not by anyone. Let her go."

He sat there. Processing. Then nodded.

"You're right. I know you're right. But it's hard. Being a parent. Letting go when everything in you says hold on."

"Can't imagine."

"No. You can't. But you did your best. Got her out. That's more than I deserved after being absent her whole life."

He pulled out an envelope. Put it on my desk.

"What's this?"

"Final payment. Bonus actually. For everything you went through. Everything you lost."

"I don't want it."

"Take it anyway. I don't want it either. Money from my last gig. Reunion show. Blood money from nostalgia. Better in your hands than mine."

I took it. Didn't open it. Put it in the drawer with the first payment. Next to where the Jameson used to be.

"How are you doing?" he asked. "Really."

"Sober. Forty-two days now. Going to meetings. Doing the work."

"That's good."

"And guilty. And damaged. And questioning everything. But sober."

"Yeah. That sounds about right." He stood. "There's a meeting tonight. Tuesday night. Koreatown. Same place we used to go. I'll be there. If you want."

"Maybe."

"Maybe's better than no." He walked to the door. Stopped. "Thank you, Blair. I know it cost you. I know you're carrying shit from this you'll never put down. But you tried. You cared. That matters. Even when it doesn't feel like it matters."

He left.

I sat there. Looked at the envelope. The case file with Siobhan's photo. The empty space where the bottle used to be.

My phone rang. Torres.

"Blair. Got news."

"Good or bad?"

"Depends. Emmett took a plea. Twenty years. No trial. He flipped on his suppliers in exchange for reduced time. Could be out in twelve with good behavior."

"Okay."

"You sound disappointed."

"I don't know what I sound like anymore."

"There's more. The house. The Venice property. It's being auctioned. City's seizing it. Selling it to recover costs."

"Good for the city."

"Ramirez bought it."

"What?"

"Ramirez. The social worker. She pooled money with other advocates. Bought the property. They're turning it into a legitimate shelter. No cult. No exploitation. Just housing and services for homeless people. She wanted you to know."

Something loosened in my chest. Small thing. But something.

"That's good."

"Yeah. Thought you'd want to hear. Some good coming from all this. Some light."

"Thanks, Torres."

"You doing okay? Really?"

"Define okay."

"Fair enough. Listen. I've got a case. Missing person. Teenager. Parents are frantic. Could use an investigator who's good at finding people who don't want to be found. Interested?"

Was I?

"I don't know. After the last one..."

"I get it. But Blair? You're good at this. Better than you think. What happened with Siobhan—it's complicated. But you did find her. You did get her out. The rest is on her. On Emmett. On the world. Not on you."

"Feels like it's on me."

"I know. But it's not. So think about it. The case. Could use you."

"I'll think about it."

"Good. Call me."

She hung up.

I sat there thinking about new cases. New people to find. New families to break or save or something in between.

Thought about whether I could do it again.

Whether I should.

My sponsor Lonnie had said at last night's meeting: "We keep showing up. Even when we don't want to. Especially when we don't want to. That's the program. That's life. We show up."

I'd shown up to the meeting. Forty-two days sober. Small victory. Hollow but real.

Around noon, someone knocked on my office door.

"Come in."

Jason walked in.

The kid from the house. The one who'd looked at me with devastation the night of the raid.

"Jason."

"Blair. Or Pete. Whatever your name is."

"Blair. Pete was someone I pretended to be."

"Yeah." He stood there. Awkward. Angry. Lost. "Can I sit?"

"Sure."

He sat in the wobbling chair. Looked around the office. Saw the poverty. The failure. The small-time operation.

"This is where you work?"

"Yeah."

"It's shitty."

"Yeah."

He almost smiled. "You came from this to our family. Pretended to be us. While the whole time you had this to come back to. Why?"

"Because someone hired me. Because I needed the money. Because it was my job."

"That's it? Just a job?"

"At first. Then it became something else."

"What?"

"Guilt. Obligation. Maybe a little bit of wanting what you had. The belonging."

He looked at me hard. "You destroyed us. You know that, right? We were family. Real family. Then you came in and ripped it apart. Rachel tried to kill herself. Marcus is back on the street. I'm crashing at different shelters every night.

Siobhan's gone. Everyone's scattered. Because of you."

"I know."

"And you're okay with that?"

"No. I'm not okay with anything."

"Good." He leaned back. "I came here to hate you. To tell you what you did. To make you feel as bad as we all feel."

"Did it work?"

"I already felt that bad."

We sat there. Two broken people in a shitty office. Connected by lies and betrayal and the ruins of something that had been real and false at the same time.

"Emmett was using you," I said. "Using all of you. The drugs. The prostitution. The exploitation. That wasn't family. That was business."

"I know. The counselors explained it. Showed us the pattern. Told us we were victims. But you know what? I don't care. I'd rather be a used member of a family than a free person with nothing. At least I had purpose. At least I mattered."

"You matter now. You're alive. You're free. You can build something real. Something that's not based on lies."

"Can I? Because I don't know how. Don't know how to live without the structure. Without the purpose. Without the family." His voice cracked. "You took that from me. And I don't know how to get it back."

I didn't have answers. Didn't have wisdom. Didn't have anything except my own guilt and the knowledge that he was right.

"I'm sorry," I said. "For what it's worth. I'm sorry I destroyed what you had. Sorry I couldn't think of a better way. Sorry I'm not the person you needed me to be."

He wiped his eyes. Stood up.

"I came here to hate you. But I can't. Because you're just as lost as the rest of us. Just as broken. Just as desperate for something to believe in."

"Yeah."

"So I don't forgive you. But I understand you. And maybe that's worse."

He walked to the door. Stopped.

"If you hear about Siobhan. If she contacts you or you find out where she is. Tell me? Not Declan. Not the cops. Me. Just so I know she's okay."

"I will."

"Thanks."

He left.

I sat there alone again.

Thought about what he said. About being just as lost. Just as broken.

He wasn't wrong.

That evening I drove to Venice Beach.

Hadn't been back since the raid. Avoided it. The memories. The guilt. The ghosts.

But something pulled me there.

Parked near the canals. Walked to where the house had been. Where Ramirez was building the shelter.

Construction was underway. The structure being renovated. Made legitimate. Made clean.

Ramirez was there. Supervising. Saw me. Walked over.

"Blair."

"Ramirez."

"Heard you might come by. Torres said you'd been avoiding Venice."

"Yeah."

"Don't blame you. This place has memories."

We stood there looking at the work. The transformation.

"What you're doing here," I said. "It's good. Important."

"Trying to save what could be saved. The idea of community. Of helping people. Just without the exploitation. Without the lies."

"You think it'll work?"

"Don't know. But we're trying. That's all you can do. Try and hope it's enough."

She looked at me. "You did the right thing. Stopping Emmett. Exposing the operation. I know it doesn't feel that way. But you did."

"Everyone keeps saying that."

"Because it's true. And because we know you're drowning in guilt. We're trying to throw you a line."

"Not sure I want to grab it."

"Grab it anyway. Drown later if you have to. But at least try to swim first."

She went back to the construction. Left me standing there.

I walked to the boardwalk. The ocean was gray. The tourists were gone. Just locals now. Evening settling in.

Found a bench. Sat down.

Watched the water. Watched the sky. Watched Venice being Venice. Selling dreams and breaking hearts and surviving despite everything.

My phone buzzed. Text from unknown number.

*I'm okay. Don't look for me. Tell my dad I'm okay but I need time. Years maybe. Tell him I'm sorry but I can't see him. Can't see any of it. Tell him to let me go. -S*

Siobhan.

I texted back: *Will tell him. Take care of yourself.*

No response.

Didn't expect one.

I called Declan. Told him. He cried. Thanked me. Hung up.

Sat there as the sun went down.

Thought about endings. About the difference between resolution and conclusion. About how most things don't resolve. They just stop.

This wasn't resolved. Siobhan was gone. The family was scattered. Emmett was in prison. Rachel was in recovery. Jason was lost. Marcus was on the streets again.

Nothing fixed.

Nothing healed.

Nothing made right.

Just ended.

And somehow life kept going anyway.

I stood up. Walked back to my car.

Drove to the meeting in Koreatown.

Sat in the back. Listened to people share. Heard Declan talk about letting go. Heard Lonnie talk about acceptance. Heard strangers talk about survival.

Didn't share. Just listened.

After, Lonnie found me.

"Forty-two days. That's good."

"Doesn't feel good."

"Never does. But it is. You're here. You're sober. You're trying. That's all any of us can do."

"Is it enough?"

"It has to be. Because it's all we've got."

We stood outside the church. The city spreading out around us. Vast and indifferent and full of people trying to survive their own damage.

"What now?" I asked.

"Now you keep going. One day at a time. Take the case Torres offered. Or don't. Help people. Or don't. But keep showing up. Keep trying. Keep being Peter Blair even when you don't remember who that is."

"And if I fail?"

"Then you fail. And then you try again. That's the program. That's life. We fail and we try again until we can't anymore. Then we die. But until then, we keep trying."

He clapped my shoulder. Walked to his car.

I stood there. Alone with the city and the night and the weight of everything I'd done and failed to do.

Thought about Ken Bruen. About Jack Taylor. About damaged men trying to do right in a wrong world. About how they kept failing and kept trying and kept surviving despite everything.

I wasn't Jack Taylor.

Wasn't a character in a noir novel.

Was just Peter Blair. Forty-two days sober. One case finished. One catastrophe survived. One life still somehow continuing.

I got in my car.

Drove back to Echo Park.

Back to my apartment. My books. My coffee maker. My small life.

Tomorrow I'd call Torres.

Maybe I'd take a new case. Maybe not.

Tomorrow I'd go to another meeting.

Keep the streak alive. Keep trying.

Tomorrow I'd try to be better than I was today.

But tonight I just sat at my window.

Watched the city lights.

Drank coffee black and bitter.

Thought about Siobhan. About Declan. About Rachel and Jason and Marcus and everyone I'd saved and destroyed and failed and helped in equal measure.

Thought about the family I'd broken.

The community I'd scattered.

The price of doing the right thing.

There was a new case file on my desk. The one Torres mentioned. Missing teenager. Desperate parents.

I looked at it.

Thought about opening it.

Thought about diving back in. Finding people. Breaking families. Saving lives. Destroying worlds.

Not tonight.

Tonight I just sat there.

Surviving.

That was enough.

It had to be.

The city kept moving. Kept selling. Kept breaking hearts.

And I kept sitting.

Kept breathing.

Kept being Peter Blair.

Whoever that was.

The Venice Beach Psalms were over.

The congregation scattered.

The prophet imprisoned.
The lost girl gone again.
And me?
I was still here.
Still damaged.
Still trying.
Still somehow alive.
Los Angeles spread out below my window.
Dark with something more than night.
But morning would come.
It always did.
And when it came, I'd still be here.
Making coffee.
Going to meetings.
Trying to remember who I was.
Trying to forget what I'd done.
Trying.
Always trying.
That was the job.
That was the life.
That was all there was.
I lit a cigarette.
Looked out at the city.
And waited for tomorrow.
Whatever it brought.